Acclaim for *The 25th Hour*

"As unusual as it is well wrought: it r[...]
sense of the city's possibilities a[...]
—*The New [...]*

"Exciting . . . intriguing."
—*Chicago Tribune*

"*The 25th Hour* shines. It couldn't get much better."
—*San Francisco Chronicle*

"Remarkable . . . Each chapter stands in jewel-like clarity,
and the novel feels like a darkly introspective movie . . .
The relationships [are] flawed and real . . . A human novel that
ends up being more about hope than about cynicism."
—*The Denver Post*

"The kind of tough, honest, young-in-New York novel you're
always looking for but seldom seem to find. A story that will
engage your mind and trigger your pulse from beginning to end."
—George P. Pelecanos, author of *Hell to Pay*

"David Benioff has written a terrific first novel. The predicament
he creates for his protagonist holds us to the end."
—Vincent Patrick, author of
The Pope of Greenwich Village

"A riveting account of neither crime nor punishment, but the
hellish, temporary suspension between those two worlds. This
book is at once brutal and beautiful. I could not put it down."
—Ann Patchett, author of *Bel Canto*

THE 25th HOUR

BY
DAVID BENIOFF

A PLUME BOOK

PLUME
Published by the Penguin Group
Penguin Putnam Inc., 375 Hudson Street, New York, New York 10014, U.S.A.
Penguin Books Ltd, 80 Strand, London WC2R 0RL, England
Penguin Books Australia Ltd, Ringwood, Victoria, Australia
Penguin Books Canada Ltd, 10 Alcorn Avenue, Toronto, Ontario, Canada M4V 3B2
Penguin Books (N.Z.) Ltd, 182–190 Wairau Road, Auckland 10, New Zealand

Penguin Books Ltd, Registered Offices: Harmondsworth, Middlesex, England

Published by Plume, a member of Penguin Putnam Inc. Published by arrangement with Carroll & Graf
Publishers, Inc., a Division of Avalon Publishing Group. For information address Carroll & Graf Publishers,
Inc., 19 West 21st Street, New York, New York 10010-6805.

First Plume Printing (movie tie-in), November 2002
10 9 8 7 6 5 4 3 2 1

Lyrics from "Up Against the Wall, Redneck" © 1974 by Ray Wylie Hubbard reprinted by permission of
Tennessee Swamp Fox Music Company. All rights controlled and administered by EMI Blackwood Inc.
International copyright secured.

 REGISTERED TRADEMARK—MARCA REGISTRADA

LIBRARY OF CONGRESS CATALOGING-IN-PUBLICATION DATA:

Benioff, David.
The 25th hour / David Benioff.

p. cm.
ISBN 0-452-28295-0
ISBN 0-452-28419-8 (movie tie-in)
1. New York (N.Y.)—Fiction.   2. Drug traffic—Fiction.   3. Revenge—Fiction.   1. Title.
Twenty-fifth hour.   II. Title.

PS3552.E54425 A613 2001
813'.6—dc21   2001052341

Printed in the United States of America

PUBLISHER'S NOTE
This is a work of fiction. Names, characters, places, and incidents either are the product of the author's imag-
ination or are used fictitiously, and any resemblance to actual persons, living or dead, business establishments,
events, or locales is entirely coincidental.

BOOKS ARE AVAILABLE AT QUANTITY DISCOUNTS WHEN USED TO PROMOTE PRODUCTS OR SERVICES. FOR
INFORMATION PLEASE WRITE TO PREMIUM MARKETING DIVISION, PENGUIN PUTNAM INC., 375 HUDSON
STREET, NEW YORK, NEW YORK 10014.

For Mom and Dad—
thank you.

THE 25th HOUR

PROLOGUE

THEY FOUND THE black dog sleeping on the shoulder of the West Side Highway, dreaming dog dreams. A crippled castoff, left ear chewed to mince, hide scored with dozens of cigarette burns—a fighting dog abandoned to the mercy of river rats. Traffic rumbled past: vans with padlocked rear doors, white limousines with tinted glass and New Jersey plates, yellow cabs, blue police cruisers.

Monty parked his Corvette on the shoulder and shut off the engine. He stepped from the car and walked over to the dog, followed by Kostya Novotny, who shook his head impatiently. Kostya was a big man. His thick white hands hung from the sleeves of his overcoat. His face had begun to blur with fat; his broad cheeks were red from the cold. He was thirty-five and looked older; Monty was twenty-three and looked younger.

"See?" said Monty. "He's alive."

"This dog, how do you call it?"

"Pit bull. Must have lost somebody some money."

"Ah, *pit bull*. In Ukraine my stepfather has such dog. Very bad dog, very bad. You have seen dogfights at Uncle Blue's?"

"No."

Flies crawled across the dog's fur, drawn by the scent of blood and shit. "What do we do, Monty, we watch him rot?"

"I was thinking of shooting him."

Awake now, the dog stared impassively into the distance, his face lit by passing headlights. The pavement by his paws was littered with broken glass, scraps of twisted metal, black rubber from blown tires. A concrete barricade behind the dog, separating north- and southbound traffic, bore the tag SANE SMITH in spray-painted letters three feet high.

"Shooting him? Are you sick in the head?"

"They just left him here to die," said Monty. "They threw him out the window and kept driving."

"Come, my friend, it is cold." A ship's horn sounded from the Hudson. "Come, people wait for us."

"They're used to waiting," said Monty. He squatted down beside the dog, inspecting the battered body, trying to determine if the left hip was broken. Monty was pale-skinned in the flickering light, his black hair combed straight back from a pronounced widow's peak. A small silver crucifix hung from a silver chain around his neck; silver rings adorned the fingers of his right hand. He leaned a little closer and the dog scrambled upright, lunged for the man's face, came close enough that Monty, stumbling frantically backward, could smell the dog's foul breath. The effort left the pit bull panting, his compact, muscular frame quivering with each rasped breath. But he remained in his crouch, watching the two men, his ears, the mangled and the good, drawn back against his skull.

"Christ," said Monty, sitting on the pavement. "He's got some bite left."

"I think he does not want to play with you. Come, you want police to pull over? You want police looking through our car?"

"Look what they did to him, Kostya. Used him for a fucking ashtray."

A passing Cadillac sped by them, honking twice, and the two men stared after it until its taillights disappeared around a bend.

Monty rose to his feet and dusted his palms on the seat of his pants. "Let's get him in the trunk."

"What?"

"There's a vet emergency room on the East Side. I like this guy."

"You like him? He tries to bite your face off. Look at him, he is meat. You want some dog, I buy you nice puppy tomorrow."

Monty was not listening. He walked back toward his car, opened the trunk, pulled out a soiled green army blanket. Kostya stared at him, holding up his hands. "Wait one second, please. Please stop one minute? I do not go near pit bull. Monty? I do not go near pit bull."

Monty shrugged. "This is a good dog. I can see it in his eyes. He's a tough little bastard."

"Yes, he is tough. He grew up in bad neighborhood. That is why I stay away from him."

The light shining down from above cast deep shadows beneath Monty's cheekbones. "Then I'll do it myself," he said.

By now the dog had slumped back to the pavement, still struggling to keep his head up, to keep his glazing eyes focused on the two men.

"Look at him," said Monty. "We wait much longer, he'll be dead."

"One minute ago you want to shoot him."

"That was a mercy thing. But he's not ready to go yet."

"Yes? He told you this? You know when he is ready to go?"

Monty carefully circled behind the dog, holding the army blanket as a matador holds his cape. "It's like a baby, they hate getting shots from the doctor. They're screaming and crying as soon as they see the needle. But in the long run, it's good for them. Here, distract him."

Kostya shook his head with the air of one who had long suffered his friend's lunacies, then kicked a soda can. The dog's eyes pivoted to follow the movement. Monty hurled the blanket over the dog and sprang forward, wrapping his arms around the dog's midsection. The dog growled and wrestled with the wool, sinking his teeth into the fabric and shaking it violently, trying to break the blanket's neck. Monty managed to stand, struggling to maintain his bear hug, but the dog, slick with blood, slithered madly in his grasp like a monstrous newborn. Monty lurched toward the Corvette as the pit bull released the blanket and turned his head, snapping viciously, his jaws inches from Monty's throat. He clawed at Monty's arms until Monty hurled him into the trunk, the dog still biting as he fell into the hollow of the spare tire, trying unsteadily to regain his footing as the lid slammed shut.

Monty picked up the army blanket and returned to the driver's seat. Kostya stared at the sky for a moment and then joined his friend in the Corvette. The entire encounter had lasted five minutes.

"What goes on in your little head?" asked Kostya, after Monty had tossed the blanket into the well behind his seat and started the car. "That was very stupid thing you did. Most stupid thing you ever did. No, I take that back. Lydia Eumanian was most stupid thing you ever did."

"I got him, didn't I?" said Monty, grinning. "A little of the tricks, a little of the quicks, *boom!* Nabbed." He checked his mirrors and pulled onto the highway, heading uptown again.

"Yes. The quicks. Meanwhile, you are bleeding. You get bit."

"No, that's the dog's blood."

Kostya raised his eyebrows. "Yes? Because you have hole in your neck and blood is coming out."

Monty lifted his hand to his neck, felt the warm dribble of blood. "Just a scratch."

"A scratch, oh. Meanwhile, you bleed to death. And you need rabies shot."

"They'll stitch it up at the vet's." Behind them the dog thrashed around in the trunk, his bellows muted by the traffic.

"What? The vet? You bleed all over car, you die, your father yells at *me*. Oh, boo-hoo, boo-hoo, you let Monty die. No, please. Go to Seventh Avenue, there is Saint Something, a real hospital."

"We're going to the vet." The blood ran down Monty's arm, soaking his shirtsleeve, puddling at the elbow.

"Rule number one," said Kostya, "don't grab half-dead pit bulls.

We have people waiting for us, people with money, and you play cowboy—no, dogboy—in middle of highway. You're bad luck; you put bad luck on me. Always everything that can go wrong, goes wrong. Doyle's Law. It is not just you and me when we go out, no, no, it is Monty, Kostya, and Mister Doyle of Doyle's Law."

"Doyle? You mean Murphy."

"Who's Murphy?"

"Who's Doyle? Murphy's Law," said Monty. "Whatever can go wrong will go wrong."

"Yes," said Kostya. "Him."

From that day on the dog was Doyle.

ONE

MONTY HAS SAT on this bench a hundred times, but today he studies the view. This is his favorite spot in the city. This is what he wants to see when he closes his eyes in the place he's going: the green river, the steel bridges, the red tugboats, the stone lighthouse, the smokestacks and warehouses of Queens. This is what he wants to see when his eyes are closed, tomorrow night and every night after for seven years; this is what he wants to see when the electronically controlled gates have slammed shut, when the fluorescent lights go down and the dim red security lights go up, during the nighttime chorus of whispered jokes and threats, the grunts of masturbation, the low thump of heavy bass from radios played after hours against rules. Twenty-five hundred nights in Otisville, lying on a sweat-stained mattress among a thousand sleeping convicts, the closest friend ninety miles away. Green river, steel bridges, red tugboats, stone lighthouse.

Monty sits on a bench on the esplanade overlooking the East River, his right hand drumming the splintered slats, the leash wrapped tightly around his wrist. He watches Queens through the curved bars of an iron balustrade, the Triborough Bridge to the north, the 59th Street Bridge to the south. Midway across the river is the northern tip of Roosevelt Island, guarded by an old stone lighthouse.

The dog wants to run. He battles the leash, straining forward
on hind legs, coiled muscles twitching, black lips drawn back from
bright fangs. After four years of taking Doyle to the river, Monty
knows that letting him loose would bring war to the esplanade.
Maybe the pit bull would mount the Dalmatian bitch by the broken water fountain, maybe he'd brawl with the Rottweiler. No
matter, splatter the pavement with dog seed or dog blood, sound
out the vast arena with barks and yelps—Doyle is ready to go.

The river flows forty feet below man and dog, muddy green,
pierced here and there with the shimmer of aluminum soda cans.
A freshly painted red tugboat, flanks studded with truck tires, hauls
a garbage barge downstream. Seagulls circle above the barge, cursing each other, white wings translucent in the first minutes of day-
light. They dive into the waves and snatch scraps of edible trash,
swallowing with a quick jerk of the head.

Doyle squats down on the pavement and watches the other
dogs sadly, his mouth slightly ajar, his tongue leaping out now and
again. A swollen-chested pigeon, clawed feet the color of chewed
bubble gum, struts forward with bobbing head till the pit bull sends
him flying with a casual growl. Three benches away a man practices his chords on a twelve-string guitar. Two young men in
hooded sweatshirts pass by, jeans worn below their hips, green letters tattooed on their knuckles. They nod to Monty but he doesn't
notice them. He is watching the river run south, the giant smokestacks of Queens blowing white clouds skyward, the tram rising
from Roosevelt Island, the shine of traffic on the 59th Street
Bridge. A plane climbs above LaGuardia and Monty follows its as-
cent, the left wing dipping as it angles west. He is intent upon the
flight, the ease with which the silver jet speeds away.

Monty feels tension on the leash spooled around his wrist.
Doyle has risen again, to utter a sharp bark of warning at an approaching man. The newcomer stops and waits, a frightened half
smile on his face. He is not dressed for the unusual warmth of
this January morning: a long scarf looped twice around his neck,
a heavy down parka splitting at the seams, rubber boots rising

nearly to his knees. He steps from foot to foot, chewing his gum madly.

"What's up there, Monty? You're out early today."

The plane has disappeared. Monty nods but does not speak.

"You want to tell the dog to relax? Hey there, pooch. Hey, good dog. I don't think your dog likes me."

"Go away, Simon."

The man nods, rubbing his hands together. "I'm hungry here, Monty. Woke up an hour ago, and I was hungry."

"Nothing I can do about that. Go up to a Hundred and Tenth."

"A Hundred and Tenth? Come on, I'm good." He reaches into his pocket and brings out a wad of five-dollar bills held together by a rubber band.

"Put that away," snaps Monty, and Doyle snarls.

"Okay, okay. I'm just saying I'm not looking for a mercy pop."

Monty stares at the lighthouse across the river. "I'm over, man."

Simon points to a trail of small scabs along his throat. "Look at this. Cut myself shaving this morning—four times! I can't keep my hands steady. Come on, Monty. Help me out here. I can't go to Harlem—look at me. Who do I know in Harlem? They'll gut me up there. I'll be like Jerry running from Tom. Need my cheese, Monty, need my cheese! I'm starving, man."

There is a long silence and then Monty stands and walks toward the man, closer and closer until their faces are inches apart. "You need to leave me alone, friend. I told you, I'm out of business."

Doyle sniffs at Simon's boots, then raises his head, snout climbing the man's leg. Simon dances a half step, trying to keep away from the dog without startling him. "What are you talking about? You worried about me narking you out? Look at me, man. You know who I am."

"You're not listening to me. I got touched. Game over. So back off and go home to your lawyer mother or go to a Hundred and Tenth Street, whatever you want. Just leave me the fuck alone."

Simon blinks and stumbles backward, tries to laugh, looks behind him, looks down at Doyle, rubs his nose with the back of his hand. "Five years I've been coming to you. All right, no problem. I'll leave. There's no need to be nasty."

The dog is anxious to move; he tugs at his leash and Monty follows him past the concrete chessboards where the two of them have stood in the summer crowds, watching the duels. Little Vic used to play here; Little Vic who had been grand master at Riker's Island until a Russian got busted on forgery charges and demolished him in four straight games. But no hustlers punch their chess clocks today; too early on a winter's morning. The rubes are all home eating breakfast.

Monty and Doyle walk west, pausing behind a fence to watch a basketball game, the teenage players taking advantage of the warm air, one last game before school. Doyle sniffs posts that stink of yesterday's piss. Monty assesses the ballers quickly, accurately, and disdainfully. The point can't make an entry pass to save his life; the two guard has no left; the big man down low telegraphs his every shot. Monty remembers a Saturday when he and four friends owned this court, won game after game after game until the losers stumbled away in frustration, an August afternoon when every jump shot was automatic, when he could locate his teammates with his eyes closed and slip them the ball as easy as kissing the bride.

Man and dog walk down a cascading series of steps into the courtyard of Carl Schurz Park. A square of black bars encloses two rows of stunted gingko trees, their leaves shaped like Japanese fans. Old people, enjoying the weather, gather on the benches that line the gated plot, throwing crumbs to the birds, reading the back pages of the *Post*, chewing potato knishes. Black women push white babies in plastic strollers. Jagged boulders scrawled with paint serve as markers on the slopes surrounding the courtyard: MIKO+LIZ; 84 BOYS; THE LOWLITE CRUZERS; SANE SMITH. Sane Smith was here. Sane Smith was everywhere. Sane Smith is dead, having jumped from the Brooklyn Bridge. At least that was what Monty heard. The farthest-ranging of New York graffiti artists, Sane Smith wrote his name on billboards and highway overpasses

and water tanks everywhere from Far Rockaway to Mosholu Park-
way, Sheepshead Bay to Forest Hills, New Lots to Lenox. They'll
be scrubbing his name from walls for the next hundred years.

Doyle pauses to inspect the treasures held in an orange wire-
mesh garbage can, but Monty pulls him forward. As they wait for
the light to change on East End a fire truck rumbles past, the men
on board big-boned and confident, slouched and ready in their
high boots. A rear-mount aerial ladder, thinks Monty, and he
watches the red truck disappear to the north. You could have been
a wonderful fireman, he tells himself. Instead he is here, walking
his dog in Yorkville, staring at everything, trying to absorb every
detail, the way fresh asphalt spreads like black butter across the avenue, the way taillights at dawn flash and swerve, the way bright
windows high above the street hide people he will never meet.

He passes a diner on Second Avenue. A beautiful girl seated in
a booth smiles at him, her chin propped on a menu—but it's too
late, she can no longer help. In twenty-four hours he boards a bus
for Otisville. Tomorrow at noon he surrenders his name for a
number. The beautiful girl is a curse. Her face will haunt him for
seven years.

TWO

NOSE PRESSED TO the plate-glass window, Slattery wonders how close to the Hudson a good jump would get him. Standing on the thirty-second floor—assume each floor has a ten-foot ceiling, a two-foot interstice between that ceiling and the floor above, 320 plus 64 equals 384, a 384-foot fall. And how far from the building to the river? Call it 300 feet. A 384-foot vertical, 300-foot horizontal, for a hypotenuse of . . . Slattery frowns. Wait a second. A jump out this window will not be a slide down the hypotenuse. Gravity will suck him earthward as soon as he loses momentum. So, a leap of 300 feet.

First he would have to break through the glass with a chair. Position the starting line by the water cooler on the far wall; that gives him a twenty-yard sprint. Timing the jump is critical: a moment too early or too late and his foot fails to clear the window frame, leaving him toppling shame-faced over the edge, catcalls and laughter the last sounds he hears.

Not that it matters, thinks Slattery. He could run his fastest, jump at the perfect moment, catch a strong tail wind—the river is too far. He would never reach water, never come close. Instead his effort would end, colorfully, on gray concrete. The pedestrians below would remember the arc of his fall, the curious pumping motion of his legs, mimicking Olympic long jumpers. But it's hopeless, leaping for the Hudson. Moments after impact, the traders, clustered around the broken window, would return to their desks, begin composing their jokes. Within minutes, all of Manhattan's investment bankers would know the story, reduced to a blurb, compact and honed for a supper recounting among family and friends: Slattery splattery.

He bangs his head softly against the glass, then straightens up. All this morbid fantasizing might be premature. After all, he argues with himself, he owns the highest batting average on the floor. None of the other traders in his department has gathered so much loot for the firm. Discounting the misadventures of early July, that succession of horrid maneuvers (and what slugger does not suffer a seasonal slump?), discounting that fortnight and Slattery is the local star, a true-blue rainmaker, the Hank Aaron of the thirty-second floor. It doesn't matter, he tells himself. One hour from now it will all be over.

A pale blue light arcs over the black river as the sun rises behind Slattery and reluctantly begins to illuminate the Jersey shore. Rising over Brooklyn, he thinks, rapping the glass with his knuckles. Screw this deal up and I'm going back to Brooklyn, say goodbye to the West Village apartment, hello again Mom, Dad, Eoin, and Aunt Orla from County fucking Wicklow, that witch, with her inside information on every situation planet-wide. Any disturbance between men that has ever occurred in the world's turbulent history, Aunt Orla has her bitter opinions. Mention an agrarian dispute in ancient Sumeria, Orla chooses her side by the third word; she'll be spitting maledictions at the enemy, the eejits, chanting benedictions for the aggrieved ally, the poor lambs, and claiming distant relations amongst that flock, the Akkadians or whatnot, and weren't they the long-suffering Irish of Mesopotamia?

Every transaction, for Slattery, is a choice between two closed doors. Turn the wrong knob and the trap is sprung, fall back into Bay Ridge to bunk with a dim-witted little brother and breakfast with the endlessly irate Orla, the thirty-second floor a fast-fading mirage, and Dad clapping his hand to your back, telling you not to worry, a union card's a cinch what with a crane operator for a cousin.

Slattery returns to his desk and sits with his hands behind his head, staring at the rows of numbers marching across the screens of his seven monitors. He taps a few keys and the numbers of one column freeze, today's close in the Hong Kong market. Slattery rubs the bottom of his chin with a clenched fist and looks to the clocks fixed on the wall, the precise minute in Tokyo, Hong Kong, Frankfurt, London, New York: 7:57 here on the Eastern Seaboard. Half an hour till the number comes out. The trading floor hums, the low and nervous murmur of every month's final Thursday. Big money to be made today, big money to be lost.

Slattery's eyes are undercast with black crescents. He wakes each morning at five-thirty and rides ten imaginary miles on his stationary bike. An hour later he arrives at the office, seats himself before his array of electronics, and scans his seven screens for information, for clues he might have missed the previous afternoon.

The brown curls have begun their slow retreat from his forehead. An ex-wrestler, Slattery's nose has been broken four times, his ears cauliflowered, his front teeth chipped from an accidental head butt sophomore year of college. His neck remains massive from grappling days, out of proportion to the rest of his body. He hasn't been able to fasten the top button of his dress shirts since high school.

"Coming out with us later on?"

Slattery looks up from his monitors and nods at his supervisor, the man who hired him four years ago: Ari Lichter, plump face flushed after walking three blocks from the subway station, cloaked in his winter overcoat though the morning is unseasonably warm.

"You owe me ten bucks," says Slattery.

"And good morning to you." Lichter thumbs through his wallet, finds a ten-dollar bill, hands it over. "I don't want you to break my thumbs."

"Thank you, boss. Never bet on the Sixers, they're uncoachable." Slattery snaps the bill taut between his fingers. "A little warm for that coat, isn't it?"

"Supposed to get some snow later on. If you want to start spending that big money, people are getting together at Sobie's after work, watch the Knicks game."

"Sobie's?" Slattery eyes his boss skeptically. "You still trying for that bartender?"

"I like the place. Good beer."

"Oh, yeah, they've got the best Budweiser in town. That girl can't be twenty years old. She could be your daughter, boss."

Lichter shakes his head. "Listen, my young friend, I'm a fat, happy suburban dad. And I follow the rules. But I'm allowed to look."

"Give me a report tomorrow," says Slattery. "I'm going out with some friends tonight."

"Big date?"

"Nah, not even. Sort of a going-away party."

Mentioning his plans for the night makes Slattery uneasy. So far this morning he has managed to keep thoughts of Monty buried beneath the numbers, the constant calculations and recalculations of his gamble. He wonders what his friend is planning to do with Doyle. The two have been inseparable since Monty found the dog four years ago; Monty has a hard time sleeping when the pit bull isn't curled up outside the bedroom door. Bad enough to lock a man in a cell, to take him from his family, his friends, his city—couldn't he at least keep his dog? If Monty had Doyle to lick his face in the morning, Doyle to bark in warning whenever a stranger approached, Doyle just sitting, quiet and content, head on the floor between his paws, brown-eyed and watching—maybe it would make seven years pass a little quicker.

"The other thing," says Lichter. "You're still holding on to all those contracts?"

"Yeah. Why, you're nervous?"

"I don't like it," says Lichter. "The claims numbers have dropped three weeks straight."

"And everybody's thinking, therefore, if claims have dropped, employment must be up."

"They probably think that," says Lichter, "because it's pretty much always true."

Slattery wags his finger at his supervisor. "Pretty much always. But not this time. I've got a theory."

"Oh, good, you've got a theory. Everybody alive's got a theory, Frank. How to beat the blackjack dealer, how to pick a horse, how to ace the stock market. I've got a theory too. You want to hear it? My theory is called Theories Are Bullshit. Do me a favor. Cut your stake in half, okay?"

"You want me to sell five hundred contracts?"

"Five hundred? You've got a thousand?"

Slattery nods slowly. "Right, boss. You're quick with the numbers."

"At a hundred thousand a pop? Frank, come on, man, you're in awfully deep."

"What? They authorized me to a hundred mil. You want to—"

"A week ago," says Lichter. "They raise your limit one week ago, and you're already maxing out."

"So what's the point of giving me a limit if they don't want me to go there?"

"Listen to me. Cut your stake in half. All right? You've been doing a great job, everyone knows that. They're watching you. I'll probably be fetching your coffee in a few months. But right now I'm still your supervisor and I'm telling you: sell those contracts." He grips Slattery's shoulder, then walks toward his office, exchanging good mornings with the other traders on the floor.

Marcuse peeks his head over the partition facing Slattery. "Better hop to, sonny boy."

Slattery says nothing, stabbing angrily at his keyboard, calling forth further tables and figures. But Marcuse remains, chin resting on the partition like a latter-day Kilroy. "I don't see you picking up the phone," he says. "Didn't Lichter just tell you to sell? Sounds like your allowance got cut off."

Slattery narrows his eyes but continues to peruse the screens, refusing to acknowledge the taunts. Marcuse, far from being deterred, continues. "You're not going to disobey a direct order, are you? That could get you thrown in the brig. They'll have you on KP duty for years."

"You want to back off and let me work? Okay? I don't come into your bedroom and tell you how to fuck your wife, do I?"

Marcuse mimes wiping a tear from his eye. "I thought you liked my wife."

"I do like your wife. The fact that she married you is a big strike against her."

"Getting a little testy, huh, Frank? Hey, I'm on your side. We're all working for the same team, right?"

Slattery rolls backward in his chair and looks up at Marcuse. "I've got work to do, so do me a favor, would you? Just do me a favor and shut up. Whatever happens, happens; it's got nothing to do with you."

"You got it, Frank," says Marcuse, winking. "Give 'em hell."

If it all goes sour, thinks Slattery, I will jump that partition, break three of his ribs, and console myself pummeling him till the security guards arrive and throw me out the door. The others on the floor would never interfere. Marcuse is widely detested, from the receptionists to the vice presidents, though redeemed in the eyes of the firm as a proven profit maker. If Charlie Manson showed a knack for picking stocks or trading bonds, every house on Wall Street would lure him with extravagant offers.

Slattery closes his eyes and pinches the bridge of his nose. He knows this is fatal—*never allow personalities to distract you from a numbers game*—but how do you ignore a Marcuse, a man convinced that his rise depends upon Slattery's fall? It would be so much easier to leap over the partition, seize him by the throat, demand respect. A little violence to alleviate the pressures of civilized behavior, that's all.

Slattery has a hard time letting things go. At night he often dreams of avenging slanders real or imagined, wakes with a feeling of satisfaction, of justice, only to realize that the vindication is mere fantasy, the wrongs still unrighted. All the men he has not fought but should have. One time when Slattery was drinking at closing hour, a bouncer said, "Time's up. Out."

"Let me just finish my beer."

The bouncer knocked the glass from Slattery's hand. "You're finished." Two other large men came over, flanking their co-worker.

"What the fuck was that for?" asked Slattery.

"Do something," said the bouncer. Slattery did nothing. He left the bar and walked home and has been cursing himself ever since.

Or the mad-eyed man on the R train, who cursed when Slattery accidentally stepped on the man's foot. Slattery had promptly apologized but the man thrust his damp face inches from Slattery's eyes. "You want to throw with *me*, motherfucker? You want to throw with *me*?" Slattery had turned and walked away and the man hollered at his back, "That's what I thought, motherfucker. You better run!"

That was ten years ago. Slattery was seventeen. Any rational New Yorker would have walked away from that fight—*never brawl on the subway: never brawl with a lunatic*—but Slattery is unconsoled by his rationality. He replays the encounter in his mind time after time, imagining the perfect response—the perfect right hook, the perfect double-leg takedown, the perfect head butt. But the mad-eyed man is gone, untouchable.

What Slattery wants is a ring painted on concrete in the empty desert. With no living spectator around for miles, just him and the grinning demons. A chance to fight them each, one by one—the bouncer, the mad-eyed man, all of them—to leave them broken and humbled, or even to lose the fights, but with nobility, and earn the respect of all the men who have showed him none. I want peace, he thinks to himself late at night. I want peace. But then he dreams of fistfights.

Even in the cool, sterile environment of the bank's offices, these brute reveries disturb his concentration. By force of will he returns to the numbers, the endless quotes and codes of money abstracted. Working out the odds, calculating the percentages, slicing and dicing—you begin to forget the immensity of the transaction, that every fractional uptick or downtick represents a mansion by the Englewood cliffs. Slattery has no time for such considerations. Start admiring the vastness of the forest and a tree will surely fall on you, bashing your skull for the crime of perspective.

Slattery considers himself a code-breaker, spends his hours deciphering the endlessly scrolling information. Market performance, rate of inflation, economists' predictions, politicians' pronouncements, inventories, weather conditions, consumer mood swings—all play a role in determining the outcome. As a scholar of Cabala peruses the books of Moses, certain that a world of prophecy is contained within every letter, so Slattery scrutinizes his own chosen text. He refuses to believe that any other interpretation of the numbers can be valid. No one else is privy to his calculations, his formulae, his elaborate system for devising predictions.

Phelan, a new kid, eight months out of college, walks by with a cup of coffee, waving a fax sheet. "Sollie's looking for a big number, two hundred, maybe two-twenty. That's the word."

"Fuck Sollie," says Slattery.

Phelan pauses, blinks, looks down at the fax sheet and back at Slattery. "Fuck Sollie?"

"Nobody's looking to do us any favors, Phelan. They don't give us anything they think we can use. You're wearing a striped shirt and a striped tie."

Phelan examines his outfit. "Yeah? Is that bad?"

"You look like a fucking optical illusion. Go away."

At eight-twenty the futures trading begins. The floor becomes frantic with activity, everyone barking orders into their phones, calling up numbers on computer screens, stealing quick glances at the bow-tied reporter on the television, the man who will release the employment number. Slattery picks up a telephone and begins speaking to the dial tone.

"Slattery!" Lichter stands in the doorway of his office, a real of-fice with walls and windows. "We're good?"

Slattery nods and gives the thumbs-up, continuing his bogus conversation. If the number comes out two-twenty, he calculates, we're losing one and a half million. The equivalent of his father's total career earnings, forty years' wages, evaporated. He ignores the man on television reading from his script. The number will appear on Slattery's primary monitor the second it is known. He stretches his left leg and feels the cartilage creaking; he hangs up the phone and waits.

Marcuse pops his head up again and Slattery longs to club the miserable bastard like a baby seal. "Good thing you got rid of those suckers. Looks like a huge number on the way."

"You want to bet on that?"

Marcuse smiles broadly. "I think we already have."

"A little side wager, just you and me."

"How much are we talking about?"

"I don't want your money," says Slattery. "The loser has to shine the winner's shoes, right here on the trading floor, every Monday for the month of February. In front of everybody. Down on your knees, shining my shoes."

"For the whole month?"

"You can handle it; it's the shortest month of the year. In or out?"

Marcuse considers for a moment, chewing on his pencil's eraser. "What's the high low?"

"Call it one-ninety."

"Mm, no. I could see one-eighty-five."

Slattery shakes his head. "You're a cocksucker, Marcuse. You're looking two, two-twenty, and you know it. Fine, call it one-eighty-five."

Marcuse grins, extends his hand, and Slattery shakes, completely aware that he's acting like an imbecile. *Never gamble angry.* Slattery wipes his monitors clean with a tissue, taps the side of his keyboard. He closes his eyes and wills a low number. One-ninety I'm fine, even if I lose this stupid bet. I'll take a loss but it won't be a bad loss; Lichter will chew me out but it won't be a bad chewing out. Two-twenty and I'll be lifting girders from the cab of my crane come summertime.

A commotion of shouts and groans riles the floor. Slattery opens his eyes and stares at his monitor, blinks, and checks the television screen for confirmation. From behind the partition he hears Marcuse hollering into his phone. Across the floor someone yells, "Stop out of that, Schultz, get the fuck out!" And someone else: "We're going for a ride!"

In the month of January, one hundred and thirty-eight thousand new jobs were created, some seventy thousand fewer than had been predicted. Slattery watches his computer screen, dazed, as the treasury prices gap up, screaming forward without stopping for breath. In nine minutes the bond contract jumps two points. Slattery makes a phone call and leans back in his chair, swallowing hard. One thousand contracts at one hundred thousand dollars a pop, a one-hundred-million-dollar position. Two full points. A two-million-dollar profit in nine minutes.

He stands and sways slightly, bright points of light swarming before his eyes. He can sense Marcuse cringing behind the partition, waiting for the gloating to begin, but Slattery is too grateful, too relieved, to care about Marcuse. He walks slowly from the giant room, leaving the hysteria behind, and makes his way to the far side of the building, to the eastern-aspect windows. Brooklyn is hidden by rows of tall buildings but Slattery knows it's out there, coiled and waiting. He closes his eyes and kisses the plate glass.

THREE

THE TURKS USED to strap metal baskets on the crotches of their war prisoners. With a live rat in the basket. Can you picture it? What's a rat to do? He chews his way to freedom, chews through scrotum, sinew, fat. Imagine his gut-wet head peeking up from the prisoner's belly. Imagine that." LoBianco laughs. "Nobody wanted to wage war with the Turks."

Jakob marks a 73 in red ink on top of a vocabulary quiz and copies the number into his grade book. He checks his watch, caps his pen, stacks his papers on the sofa, and turns to examine LoBianco, who sits on the far side of the faculty lounge beside an unlit lamp, his gray hair cropped close to the scalp, his long earlobes dripping down toward his narrow shoulders. A bulletin board behind him is posted with announcements: department meetings, requests for dance chaperones, reminders of bus duty, the weekly lunch schedule.

"Why are you sitting in the dark?" Jakob asks.

"To prevent me from reading," says LoBianco, brandishing a sheaf of blue-book student essays. "One more paragraph about the heroism of Atticus Finch and I'll have an aneurysm." He sighs. "Thirty years I've taught that book. I'd like to sic the Turks on Harper Lee. That would be something to see. I'm sure they had special techniques for the women."

Jakob runs an untrimmed fingernail between the wales of the beige corduroy sofa. He's wearing his father's old tweed blazer, a size too large, the elbows streaked with chalk dust. Thirty years, he thinks. Thirty years divided into trimesters and school holidays, thirty years of cafeteria lunches and bad coffee, afternoon detention and faculty meetings. A lifetime segmented into periods one through eight.

Outside the lounge the bell rings and the school building surges with noise, the percussion of boot heels on linoleum, the shouts of roughhousing boys stomping down the staircase, an impromptu choir of girls in the hallway singing the theme song from a television sitcom.

"Listen," whispers LoBianco. "The little monsters are free."

"Tell me again, Anthony. Why did you become a teacher?"

"The many opportunities for child molestation."

Jakob laughs and shakes his head. "When I was a student I always wondered what you guys talked about in here. Something profound, I figured. Poetry. Deering hears you joking like that . . ." He pantomimes throat-cutting with his finger.

"They can't fire me. I'm the only one here who knows how to teach grammar."

The door swings open and a girl leans into the room, her eyes rimmed with dark makeup. "Hey, Elinsky. I have to talk to you."

"Did you hear a knock, *Mr.* Elinsky?"

"I certainly did not, Mr. LoBianco," Jakob replies.

"Miss D'Annunzio, you have not been invited to join us. Please depart."

"Jesus Christ." The door slams shut. Three knocks.

"Who's there?" asks Jakob.

"Mary."

"Mary who?" Silence. Jakob sighs. "She can't think of a punch line. Come in." Mary reenters the room and stands sullenly in the doorway. "Oh, Mary *D'Annunzio.* What a pleasant surprise."

"You have a minute, Elinsky?" She looks over at LoBianco, who clears his throat dramatically. She rolls her eyes. "*Mr.* Elinsky?"

Jakob stands, smiling. "Sure, of course. What's up?"

"I wanted to ask you about something."

"Okay. Let's go to my office. Mr. LoBianco, a cup of coffee in half an hour?"

"Let's make it an hour, Mr. Elinsky. I need to speak with Mr. Deering."

Jakob's office is a classroom he shares with another teacher. A rusted radiator gurgles under the window. Crooked words cover the blackboard—three years as an English teacher and Jakob is still incompetent with the chalk. A photograph of Mayakovski declaiming to the masses is pinned to the bulletin board above selected student writings.

"All right." Jakob seats himself on the edge of his desk, gestures Mary toward a chair. He tries to assume a stern expression but knows it's useless. LoBianco can silence a rowdy classroom with a raised eyebrow; Jakob wants to run for the door when his freshmen begin hollering and throwing paper airplanes out the windows. "What can I do for you?"

"I want to know why I got a B-plus on this story."

"Okay, first of all—"

"Nobody else in this class can write," says Mary, her fingers playing over the punk-rock band names written in silver marker on the binder she bounces on her knees. "You know it too; don't start—"

"Don't worry about everyone else. You're not competing with them."

Mary snorts. "Yeah, but I *am*, okay? I *am* competing with them. When I apply to colleges—you might have heard about this—they look at these things called grades. And if your grades aren't good—"

"Your grade will be fine. Look, Mary, why—"

"See, I don't want fine. I'm the best writer in this class. And I deserve the best grade in the class. And this, what is this? B-plus? Everyone else is writing about their fucking Christmas vacation, and you give me a B-plus?"

Mary's hazel eyes drown in pools of painted shadow, pennies

just visible at the bottom of the wishing well. Jakob wonders why she and her friends favor such a morbid style, as if their models were not chosen from the covers of slick magazines but the refrigerators of the city morgue. And her hair. When was the last time she washed her hair?

"Listen," he says, "the point is, I'm basing the grade on your own potential. Other things you've written were more carefully constructed. This one—I'm not sure it quite works."

"So what you're saying is, don't try anything new, don't experiment."

"No—"

"Because if I write something different from what you expect, I'll be punished." She rakes the blue vinyl binder cover with her glossy black nails. For one second Jakob imagines the skin of his back transposed with the vinyl.

"Punished?" He smiles. "I wouldn't call a B-plus punishment."

"Vince Miskella writes a story about his grandmother dying and you give him an A. I mean—what, you feel sorry for him, is that it? Was that a charity A? Everyone's always writing about their grandmothers dying. You know why? Not because it's so fucking traumatic. Because it's a guaranteed A. Meanwhile, the night of his grandmother's funeral, you know where Vince is? Getting drunk at a football party and slapping girls' asses. And you're all sentimental, like, 'Oh, Vince, that was very powerful, very moving.' No, it wasn't. I didn't care, you didn't care, nobody cared. That's what grandmothers do, they die. And then their grandkids write about it for school, and the teachers are forced to give them an A."

"Maybe that was Vince's way of grieving," says Jakob, trying to avoid staring at the holes in her torn jeans, at her pale knees peeking through white threading. "Sometimes guys have a hard time showing their—you know, their emotions." What am I babbling about? wonders Jakob.

"So slapping my ass, that's Vince's way of mourning his grandmother?"

Jakob glances at the open door of the classroom. All this talk of

ass-slapping is making him nervous. Mostly he wants to escape—
he knows he will never touch her, but he feels dirty anyway, an old
pervert lusting after schoolgirls. Already an old pervert at twenty-
six.

"Sometimes people get drunk because they don't want to think
about things. But," he adds, anxious not to sound like an advocate
of alcoholism, "it doesn't work. The thing you didn't want to think
about ends up being the only thing you *can* think about, and your
thoughts about it get stupider and stupider." Jakob nods twice to
affirm the logic of his comment and then tries to remember what
he just said.

"Whatever," says Mary. "The point is, this story is good. Maybe
it's not perfect, but it's better than anything anyone else handed in."

Jakob looks down at Mary's fragile wrists, one of them encir-
cled by a tattooed garland of roses. "What did your mother say
when you got that?"

"Got what?"

"Your tattoo," says Jakob, pointing.

Mary studies her wrist for a moment. "She said, 'Where'd you
get the money for that?' "

"Oh. And?"

"And what did I say or where did I get the money?"

"Well, what did you say, I guess."

"I said the guy did it for free."

"Did he?"

"No. Why do you care so much?" she asks, more surly than suspicious.

"Just curious."

"So you're not going to change the grade?"

Jakob shakes his head. "No, I'm not changing the grade."

"Great." She rises from her chair and pushes a lock of limp hair
away from her forehead. "That was a big waste of time."

"Look, instead of worrying about the grade so much, why don't
we talk about the actual story, okay? Do you have it here? I'll show
you what I thought didn't work and you can—"

"I've got rehearsal," she says, stomping out of the classroom. Jakob listens to her combat boots thumping down the hallway.

What that girl needs, thinks Jakob, staring at his own awkward scrawls on the blackboard, is a good spanking. He grins at the illegal thought.

An hour later he sits on a bar stool next to LoBianco, blowing on the head surfacing his glass of beer. It's one of the last of the vintage saloons on Amsterdam Avenue, complete with a stamped-tin ceiling, wood paneling sooted from decades of cigarette smoke, and frosted windows. Women rarely make an appearance here. Jakob supposes that the old men lounging about the room are gay, but this place is far from a pickup joint. More like a waiting room, except Jakob's not sure what they're waiting for.

"What's today," he asks, "Thursday? January's almost over. Four more months till June." Jakob wears a scuffed Yankees cap and continually tugs on the brim, like a third-base coach signaling for a hit-and-run.

"Cheers to that," says LoBianco, drinking deeply from his iced vodka. "Counting the days till summer, hmm?"

Maybe LoBianco was handsome once, but it's gone now, lost to alcohol and the pallor of a lifetime lit by fluorescent bulbs. His face rarely changes from an expression of weary disdain, as if he had just finished sneering, or was about to start sneering, or had decided that a sneer was simply too much effort to waste on the cretins surrounding him. Jakob believes the old man might have auditioned a variety of looks years ago, standing before the mirror—Withering Contempt, Half-Concealed Irritation, Condescending Amusement—and finally settled on Weary Disdain as the best of the lot.

As a former student of LoBianco's, Jakob knows how intimidating the expression can be. Students in LoBianco's classes fall into two camps: the silent masses, too fearful of mockery to speak aloud, and the courageous few, who raise their hands and daringly venture their views on the current text. The greatest reward offered to this latter group consists of LoBianco's observing the speaker for a moment, examining the ceiling, and then granting a quick nod of approval and sometimes—rarely—murmuring, "Yes, there's something to that. Interesting." Such an endorsement would make the young Jakob froth with excitement, and he would carefully transcribe his own comment into his notebook, marking it with a star to denote particular brilliance.

Jesus, what a geek, he thinks now, appraising his reflection in the mirror behind the stacked bottles of liquor, his small pointed face peering out between bars of whiskey. His own expression, he notes unhappily, suggests Nervous Agitation. I look like a ferret, he decides, a prepubescent ferret in a Yankees cap. He wrinkles his nose and bares his teeth. A definite rodent.

"Are ferrets rodents?" he asks.

"Are ferrets rodents? How did we get from June to ferrets?"

"Do you think I look like a ferret?"

LoBianco studies Jakob's face and nods. "A bit."

"A bit like a ferret. Great. Thank you." Jakob leans over the bar and picks a red plastic sword from the tray of cocktail garnishes. "So, D'Annunzio," he says, stabbing his thumb thoughtfully. "What do you think of her?"

LoBianco smiles. "What do *you* think of her, Jakob?"

"You know what? I really believe someday—I mean, maybe years from now—we'll be sitting around saying, 'I had *the* Mary D'Annunzio in my English class.' "

LoBianco is silent for a moment, tumbling ice cubes with his tongue. He demolishes them with his molars and wipes his lips. "Do you know what a man must never ask in a Victoria's Secret shop?"

"No, what?"

" 'Does this come in children's sizes?' "

Jakob feels a sudden clenching deep in his belly. "What's that supposed to mean?"

"It doesn't mean anything. It's a joke."

"What kind of joke is that?"

LoBianco reaches for his own cocktail sword and brandishes it in Jakob's face. "Have I offended your honor? You demand satis-faction? Eh? Shall we duel?"

"There's nothing going on between me and Mary D'Annun-zio."

LoBianco is not paying attention. He stabs Jakob in the leg, and the sword snaps in half.

"Ow! Ow, you bastard!"

"Shut up. Another vodka, please," LoBianco calls to the bar-tender, "and another light beer for our friend with the girlish fig-ure."

"I'm bleeding," says Jakob, examining the tiny hole in his pant leg.

"Yes, well, drink your beer and shut up." LoBianco stares at his broken sword and sighs. "We all have our problems, you know. All of us," he adds portentously.

"I guess so," mumbles Jakob. He's feeling guilty now, worrying about himself. In the morning Monty goes to prison; Jakob tries to imagine it. A judge in black robes passes sentence, and seven years are severed from a life.

"For example, wasn't today my big meeting with Deering?"

Jakob looks up. "Wasn't today your big meeting with Deering?"

LoBianco smiles. "Today was my big meeting with Deering. Do you know what he told me?" LoBianco waits, glancing at Jakob, whose attention has already wandered. "Do you?"

Jakob lowers his face to the bar, then raises it, a paper napkin stuck to his lips. He exhales and the napkin flutters to the floor. "What?"

"He told me if I had played my cards right, I could have been head of the department. Little me. Imagine that. Missed my true calling. All the power, the sheer responsibility. I could be head of the English Department—were it not that I have bad dreams."

Jakob raises his hand. "Macbeth?"

"Wrong," says LoBianco. "Delivers his philosophy lecture, the same speech I've been hearing for nineteen years now, from Socrates to William James. He has the ability to speak authoritatively on subjects of which he is entirely ignorant." LoBianco pauses, sipping his vodka. "I admire that. But his other qualities are less becoming."

"There's not going to be a punch line to this story, is there?"

"This is *not* a story"—LoBianco sniffs—"this is a rant. And I'll ask you to remain silent as you listen to it. Where was I?"

"Socrates. William James. Philosophy lecture."

"Launching from his analysis of why I failed to become department head into an unabridged history of Western Philosophy. And I just sat there with a look of polite concentration, nodding periodically and murmuring 'I see,' and 'Yes, that makes sense.' Deering placed my career stagnation in pleasant perspective. The consolations of philosophy, I suppose." LoBianco frowns, curling his fingers backward to inspect the nails, then cleaning them with the broken hilt of his cocktail sword. "I never wanted to become a man who posted *New Yorker* cartoons on his office door. But that's what I've become. If that whore Ferlinghetti hadn't—"

"Oh, no, no, no, don't—"

"That thieving bastard!" roars LoBianco. "Sitting in his landmarked bookstore, the sage of San Francisco, the last of the Beatnik poets. Poet? Poet?"

It is the great conceit of Anthony LoBianco's life that he was robbed of fame by Lawrence Ferlinghetti in 1958 in the White Horse Tavern. As the story goes, the young Anthony and his mates were drinking in that famed establishment when the Word was revealed, and Anthony, in a fever of inspiration, charged through the guzzling literati, seized a pencil and paper napkin from a startled waitress, and scribbled down his epiphany. Returning in triumph to his comrades, he held the napkin in the air and declared, "Gentlemen, I have the title for my book."

A stranger turned from his place at the bar and prodded, a bit mockingly, "So let's hear it."

"Sir," proclaimed young Anthony proudly, "*A Coney Island of the Mind*."

After informing the stranger of his title, LoBianco remembers nothing of the night; his friends apparently drowned him in whiskey to celebrate his genius. The next day he began writing his verse epic and proceeded in a fury for several months. It's very cinematic, the way LoBianco describes it, the Poet in his undershirt, unshaven, banging away at his manual typewriter in a fourth-floor walk-up on Avenue A, pausing only for cigarettes on the fire escape, where he nods in time with the saxophone blowing from across the alley, all this in black-and-white. Very Jack Kerouac. One morning the Poet returns to his apartment with a newspaper and a spinach pie from the Greek diner. Climbing up the dusty stairs he reads a headline in the middle pages, a review of a new book of poems. Written by Lawrence Ferlinghetti. Titled *A Coney Island of the Mind*. The Poet stares at the article (the headline framed nicely in a close-up) and crumples to the second-floor landing. The saxophone wails. The wondrous destiny evaporates.

It is a classical plot line of punished hubris, of gods in disguise, and Jakob enjoys it. Of course, there is one profound problem with the story—it cannot possibly be true. Jakob, investigating, discovered that Ferlinghetti got the title from a Henry Miller novel written years before the drama in the White Horse Tavern. Jakob never lets on that he has spotted the lie, partly because he thinks LoBianco has come to believe the myth and Jakob doesn't want to be cruel to the older man. But also because Jakob enjoys the secret knowledge. It gives him power over his former teacher. LoBianco, so clever in some regards, is a plain fool in others, a lousy liar, lazy in his fabrications. Jakob envisions the beaten LoBianco, consigned to oblivion, shaking his fist at a towering, deaf statue of Ferlinghetti. Christ, Anthony, you could have picked a better poet.

"You know what comforts me," asks LoBianco, "when I think of it?"

Jakob does not know.

"The man realizes he's a cheat. Every time he looks in the mirror he sees a plagiarist. Do you think he sleeps easy, that counterfeit poet? Not a chance."

Jakob thinks Ferlinghetti probably sleeps remarkably easy, but he doesn't say so.

"Deering, Deering, Deering . . . What was I on about?"

"The philosophers," says Jakob. "We're still on the philosophers."

LoBianco raises his vodka and finishes the glass, then bangs it down on the bar. "Mr. Deering, you blasphemous, righteous mouse of a man; Socrates did not die for you. Oh, there was a fine man for teaching the boys. Sure." He staggers to his feet, lifts the bar stool by its legs, mimics anal sex. "Bend over, son. Allow me to demonstrate the Socratic method. Educate all the assholes of Athens! Good man, good man. Better a sodomite than a philosopher. More fun for everyone."

Jakob, wondering why he did not leave while the leaving was good, realizes that all the middle-aged men in the room are watching this performance without expression, as if they have seen the act before, and better done.

LoBianco tries to sit but misjudges the stool's location; his knees buckle and he begins to fall. Jakob lunges for the older man, manages to catch him under the arms, and holds him upright. His hands around LoBianco's rib cage, Jakob notes how frail his old teacher has become, a tweed jacket and bones. LoBianco lives alone in his Park Slope apartment and never learned to cook. Who feeds him? wonders Jakob. He must live on takeout and free school lunches.

Shaking off Jakob's assistance, LoBianco sits heavily, facing away from the bar, and leans backward until the brass railing supports his weight. He pretends to disregard the near fall, but Jakob sees the color in his face and knows the man is embarrassed. Still, LoBianco carries on, adding volume to disguise his humiliation. "The unexamined life is not worth living, blah blah blah. True enough. But neither is the examined life; he never mentioned that."

Jakob nods, wondering if he'll be able to carry his friend to a taxi. And if a taxi driver will be willing to haul a drunkard to

Brooklyn. The bartender stands at the far end of the counter, dishrag in hand, watching LoBianco with bored irritation.

"Oh, Mr. Deering. When the plane goes down, Mr. Deering, when the babies are bawling, when the stewardesses are buckled into their seats, eyes closed and saying their prayers, when the pilot radios in his love for his wife, when the old men piss their pants and the baggage racks burst open and the suitcases tumble out and the plane is falling and the ground is rising—will your philosophy comfort you then, Mr. Deering, or will you scream with the rest of us?"

His tirade complete, LoBianco swivels about on his stool, swallows the last of his vodka, orders another. The room is silent save for the bartender pouring the drink.

"So why did he want to meet with you?" Jakob finally asks.

LoBianco watches the bartender hawkishly, suspicious that the man might pour him a short one. "Hmm? Ah, well, he's letting me go, Jakob."

"He's *what*?"

LoBianco looks up, brow wrinkled. "You can't be surprised. I've been telling you for weeks the end is near."

"But that's—how can he fire you? You're the best teacher in the department. Nobody else—"

"He's not actually firing me. He just won't renew my contract at the end of the year. I'm expensive, Jakob. They can hire one of you young pups for half the money they give me."

"That's not right, Anthony! We can't let that happen. If we get all the teachers together, we'll get everybody to sign a petition. All the students! We'll get the students, we'll get the alumni! He can't do this. No, there is no way."

"Why not? It's a private school, they can do whatever they want. Listen, it's all for the best. What should I do, teach Harper Lee until the day I die? I think not. I'll finish this year and that will be the end of it. No more blue-book essays to grade. No more vocabulary quizzes. No more red ink on my dress shirts. The schoolteacher's stigmata. Enough of that."

"But—"

"Enough, Jakob." LoBianco rises unsteadily to his feet. "Gentlemen," he calls out loudly, "raise your glasses. We have a newcomer with us today, a young man who stepped forth from the darkness into the light only minutes ago, for the first time free to indulge his true passions."

"Send him back to the darkness," comes a cry from the far corner.

"Quiet, sir. What he lacks in physical gifts he more than compensates for with . . . well, with other gifts. He's a little nervous, a bit of a virgin really, but I think you'll find him highly charming once he gets past his initial jitters."

"Why don't you shut your trap, LoBianco," yells another man. "You're not funny anymore."

This news strikes LoBianco hard, but he glares around the barroom defiantly, then snarls, "This is where faggots come to die!" He rears back as if to hurl his glass, thinks better of it, drinks deeply.

"Then die, LoBianco," says the voice from the corner, "and get it over with."

That's one way out, thinks Jakob. And the door is another.

FOUR

NATURELLE IS WAITING for Monty when he gets home, her black hair tied back in a simple braid. She sits on the stoop stairs, a closed book on her lap. When he comes closer she stands on the second step so they are eye to eye when he reaches her. They kiss, but he does not open his lips. His mouth is too dry. Doyle ferociously wags the stump of his tail and sets his front paws on the first step. Naturelle crouches down and scratches the dog behind his mangled ear and Doyle closes his eyes, licking her wrist with his rough tongue. The sun has gone down and the air's getting colder.

"You been waiting for a while?" asks Monty, drawing his keys from his pocket and mounting the steps.

"How long have you guys been walking? I woke up at seven and you were already gone."

"I didn't wear my watch." He holds the front door open for her and she passes through, Doyle bounding in behind her. "Why were you sitting down here?"

"I had my book," she says, waiting in the vestibule for Monty to open the second door. "It was a beautiful day."

Monty laughs. "Of course it was a beautiful day."

He checks the mailbox, drops a take-out menu on the tiled floor, follows his girlfriend and his dog up the dark, narrow flight of stairs. He catches hold of her hand as she reaches the landing and inspects the cover of the book she's holding. "*A Style of Her Own: The Life of Coco Chanel.* Who's she, the one with the perfume?"

"She was the Queen of Fashion. All the white ladies used to want to be white, white, white. But Coco Chanel went down to the Riviera one summer, and when she got back to Paris she had a really dark tan, and all of a sudden everybody wanted a tan."

Monty nods, half smiling, as he unlocks the four locks of his steel-plated apartment door, each turned with a separate key. The best lockpick in the five boroughs would need nearly an hour to break in; Monty knows that for a fact. They enter the apartment and Monty switches on the lights.

In contrast to the ominous staircase, the apartment is very handsome, a large one-bedroom with hardwood floors, tall windows facing the brownstones across the street, black-and-white framed photographs on the walls. Monty snapped the shots himself, mostly views of the city, with an old camera that had belonged to his father. Monty is a decent amateur, good enough that a roll of film generally produces one worthy picture. Above the sofa is a poster-size portrait of Naturelle, snarling for the camera and wielding a butcher knife. The night of that photograph she became furious because Monty continually neglected to leave messages when her mother called; she threatened to cut his heart out. She actually said, "I'll cut your heart out," yelling at him with her tiny fists clenched at her side, and he began to laugh hysterically, rolling on the floor as Doyle barked, and she started kicking him in the side, and she's small but her legs are very strong, and he would grunt and roll away from her and continue to laugh, and Doyle barked madly, confused, and finally Naturelle started to laugh too but kept kicking him in the side anyway, because he deserved it and because she didn't want him to think he was so easily forgiven, and then she ran into the kitchen and came out with the kitchen knife and yelled, "I'll cut your heart out!" while both of them laughed. "I'll do it! I'll cut your heart out and feed it to Doyle!"

Monty developed the picture himself, in a walk-in closet that his father had converted into a darkroom in his apartment in Bensonhurst. His father helped him make the frame, out of rusted metal salvaged from a junkyard. The walls of the Bensonhurst apartment are crowded with black-and-whites in rusted frames. Monty's father is a much better photographer, gifted with a discerning eye. There is a subtlety to his compositions that Monty recognizes but cannot reproduce, an ability to make the ordinary look strange. The frames are always rusted, giving the pictures the aura of relics retrieved from a sunken ship.

Monty's father had done most of the work that afternoon, sawing the metal into the necessary lengths and filing the edges smooth, while Monty drank beer and watched the football game. When the photograph was dry, and before they went out to buy the glass, Monty penciled an inscription on the back: *For Naturelle Rosario. The Day She Stole My Heart (and Fed It to My Dog)*. Later, after he had given it to her for Valentine's Day, he decided the inscription was a little goofy, even embarrassing, but Naturelle had already read it and laughed and kissed him, so it was too late for the eraser.

Today Monty does not notice the picture; it has become part of the apartment's furnishings. He unhooks Doyle's leash, and the dog trots across the room and curls up in his usual spot by the radiator. Monty turns on the television and watches the weatherman's face materialize on the screen, speaking of the coming storm. He turns off the television, looks around. Naturelle still stands by the door.

"What?" he asks.

She shrugs. "I don't know. What do you want?"

He sits down on the sofa, arms spread wide and resting on the back cushions. His feet hurt. He can feel the blisters forming on his soles, the skin raw and abraded after ten hours of walking through the city. "What do I want." He stares at Doyle for a moment. "I want to be that girl from the X-Men, the one who can walk through walls."

Naturelle walks over to the sofa and sits down next to him, her hands clasped between her legs.

"And if I can't do that," he continues, "if I can't figure out how to walk through walls, I'm thinking one shot through the roof of the mouth, *boom*, problem solved."

She hits him on the shoulder. "Quit joking about that."

"You think I'm joking?"

Naturelle stands and walks into the kitchen, pulls a jar of raw honey from the refrigerator, a teaspoon from the drying rack. She returns to the living room and sits beside Monty again, handing him the jar. "So what are we doing tonight? Before you shoot yourself."

"Uncle Blue's throwing me a party at VelVet. We ought to go." He twists off the top and gives the jar back to her. "You don't think I can do it, do you?"

"No," she says, dipping her spoon into the honey. "I know you can't. Did you meet with your probation officer today?"

"Yeah."

"What did he say?"

"He said, 'Report on time tomorrow.' " He watches her lick the teaspoon clean. "That's a nasty habit you have."

She leans over and kisses him on the lips. "Let's go into the bedroom," she says.

This is where they got him, right here, this sofa, this is where they ruined him: last June, early in the morning, awakened from a deep sleep by violent pounding on the front door and Doyle's furious barking. Naturelle, the lighter sleeper, had slipped out of bed and into a long T-shirt while the pounding continued. She left the bedroom and hushed the dog. Monty listened as she spoke to whomever was outside the door. He heard her unlock the door and open it. When she returned to the bedroom he saw her face and he thought about running, about opening the window and launching himself onto the linden tree outside, catching a branch and swinging down to the street, running as fast as he could for as long as he could. Instead he stood, pulled on a pair of sweatpants, and walked shirtless into the living room.

There were four men, all white, none much older than Monty. They wore suits with the jackets unbuttoned, shoulder holsters snug beneath each man's left armpit. They showed Monty their badges, DEA, and handed him the search papers, authorized by a federal court. All of them were smiling, so Monty smiled too, offered them coffee. They thanked him but declined.

"We're going to take a look around," Agent Brzowski told Monty, seating himself on the sofa. The other three agents strolled around the apartment. One of them crouched down by Doyle's spot next to the radiator and stroked the dog's fur. One looked out the window to the street below. The third inspected the photograph of the RCA Victor building, his hands behind his back.

"You take this picture?" he asked. When Monty said yes the agent whistled. "Nice picture. What kind of camera you got?"

Brzowski leaned back in the sofa, hands behind his head, still smiling. He listened to the conversation with interest. Naturelle headed for the bedroom but Brzowski called out to her. "Ma'am? It's Miss Rosario, right? I'm going to have to ask you to stay with us for a few minutes, okay? Can't have you wandering around out of sight."

Monty leaned against the kitchen's doorframe, willing his face to appear relaxed, free of worry. He knew how federal sentencing compared to state; state attorneys often threatened federal prosecution the way mothers scare children with stories of bogeymen. He knew it didn't matter to a federal court whether there had been prior convictions. Even with his clean record, if he got bit he was going to stay bit. But the agents weren't searching the apartment; they were looking it over as if they were appraisers from a real estate office.

"Hmm," said Brzowski, sitting up straighter. "This sofa is not very comfortable."

Monty stared at the agent and then exhaled. They were fucking with him. He was fucked.

"Maybe it's your posture," said the agent petting Doyle. "Posture's very important. You'll wind up with a bad back."

"No," said Brzowski. "It's this sofa. It's very uncomfortable. It's lumpy."

The other agents laughed and Naturelle looked at Monty. He shook his head at her and rapped the kitchen door with his knuckles. "Get it over with," he said to Brzowski.

The agent still acted bemused. "I just don't get it. It *looks* like such a nice sofa. How much did you pay for this sofa, Miss Rosario?" He stood and peered down at the cushion, stroking his chin, miming confusion. "Maybe it's the padding?"

"Could be the padding," said another agent.

Brzowski reached down and picked up the center cushion, turned it over in his hands, found the zipper. "Probably the padding." He unzipped the cushion and reached inside, pulled out handfuls of white fiber filling and let them fall to the floor like blown cotton. "Yeah, there's something *lumpy* in here, Mr. Brogan. It's a good thing I found this, you know. It'll make your sofa a whole lot more comfortable to sit on."

He pulled a package the size of a bottle of wine from the cushion, a bundle of plastic wrap and masking tape. Stray strands of fiber clung to the package like hair from a widow's scalp. Brzowski raised his eyebrows in feigned shock while the other agents oohed and clucked.

"Mr. Brogan, I do believe you're fucked."

Naturelle lies naked on her side, curled next to him, running her fingers through his hair. His back is to her, his eyes wide open. The wind blows through the windows and she shivers, presses closer to him. Monty's skin is always warm; in the depths of winter he keeps the windows open. The street noises are a lullaby for him; he grew up in a first-floor apartment.

Naturelle wonders if she will be happier when he is gone and hates herself for wondering. She remembers mornings when she woke up shivering, their naked, crooked bodies huddled together.

She would reach into the bowl of fruit kept on the nightstand, a tradition in her family, and feed him plums, or figs, or nectarines. Those were the moments she believed he really might love her, as he licked the juice from her fingers.

"Are you okay?" she asks. He says nothing and she says again, "Are you okay?"

"I'm great," he says. "Everything is wonderful. Best night of my life."

"I just want to—"

"I know," he says. "I know." He pulls his head away from her, sits up on the side of the bed, looks out the window.

"Talk to me, okay? Talk to me. Monty? Don't do this. It's our last night for—"

"It's not *our* last night. It's *my* last night. You've got tomorrow night and every other fucking night, you can go out and let some lawyer buy you drinks, you can go skinny-dipping in the Hudson, you've got all sorts of nights."

"It's still *our* last night," she says angrily, speaking to his pale, naked back. "Me and you is *our*, can't you understand that?"

"No," he says, shaking his head slowly. "Baby, do me a favor; please just be quiet. Okay?" He reaches for a pack of cigarettes and tamps it against the nightstand.

Thinking about her tomorrows makes him lonely—the idea of her laughing and talking with friends, walking down the sidewalks and glancing into shop windows, eating dinner at a restaurant. He draws a cigarette from the pack but does not light it.

Wasn't there a moment when he suspected Naturelle, a single lunatic moment when he thought *she* might have made the phone call, told them where the drugs were hidden? He had quickly slammed the door on that thought—why would she? what did she have to gain?—but once the thought is there, can you ever forget it? As soon as doubt begins to nibble at your faith, can you ever trust her again? And if you can't trust the woman who sleeps with you, the woman who lies beside you in your most unprotected hours, who can you trust?

In the distance sirens keen, and Montgomery longs to run, to bolt from the apartment, down the stairs, into the street, to catch the red truck and leap aboard with a wink for his brave comrades. He knows he could be a wonderful fireman. He wishes he were speeding toward the fire.

FIVE

THE WHORES IN the parlor love to tell stories about Uncle Blue; rolling cigarettes and sipping tea from chipped teacups, they gather in front of the fireplace and trade rumors. Every Thursday at dusk he comes to them, hangs his black coat on a hook by the door, nods to Natasha, and follows her upstairs. After the couple have cloistered themselves in the grandest room of the brownstone, proceeding in complete silence, the other women begin with the guessing, trumping each other with wilder tales. Not one of them knows his true name, though they do know that "Uncle Blue" is a corruption of his family name, a name apparently unpronounceable for Western tongues. Not one of them knows where the man comes from, though several possibilities are ventured. Perhaps he was born in a small city in Armenia, or else a village in northern Iran. Helena, a Muscovite, believes his accent is Afghani.

All of the women are émigrés from Eastern Europe, as are nearly all of their clients. The women's passage to America was facilitated by Mrs. Dimitriev, who owns the brownstone and lives in a separate apartment on the top floor, where she listens to Billie Holiday records and trades stocks on her computer, only going downstairs when there's an argument about payment.

The women arrive in the early evening and leave in the early morning. Most of them work for a year or two, until they can pay off their debt to Mrs. Dimitriev, who is so stingy she only turns on the heat in the bedrooms. So the women build big fires and drink lots of hot tea and talk. Not about work, usually—most of the johns are bores, even the dangerous ones. Uncle Blue is the exception, an enigma. The women are only certain of what they can see, so they try to frame their theories around the physical evidence. He is not a young man, though his thick hair and beard are still black. Perhaps it is the beard that reminds Helena of the Islamic fighters she remembers from childhood television, the fierce-looking men carrying AK-47s, bandoliers of ammunition crisscrossing their chests.

The skin below Uncle Blue's eyes is dark from weariness, the creases in his forehead as deep as knife scars. His palms are rough and calloused, as if from years of wielding a shovel or pick, but his fingernails are immaculate, professionally trimmed and polished. One time Natasha, staring straight into the fire, her chin held high, declared that Uncle Blue had beaten a man to death twenty years before, over a woman. She was lying, of course—if Uncle Blue *had* beaten a man to death he never would have boasted to Natasha or anyone else. Still, nobody doubts Natasha's story. After all, he has the hands of a fighting man, several fingertips splayed sideways, knuckles swollen. His wrists are as thick as Natasha's ankles.

Natasha ought to know him best, but she doesn't; she never questions him. Not that he refuses to answer, or that he forbids her from speaking—he makes no rules and has never uttered a harsh word. Uncle Blue is clean, courteous, and generous. He pays with hundred-dollar bills pulled from a silver money clip; the bills are always mint condition, the clip always full.

When he enters the house tonight she silently rises from her fireside bench and climbs the stairs to the largest bedroom. Outside is winter, the skeletal trees of Prospect Park, the streetlights crowned with yellow haloes. A dying fly buzzes feebly on the windowsill. Their transaction complete, Uncle Blue sits shirtless at the foot of the bed, forearms folded over his knees, the black spade of his beard resting on his chest. He remains in this position for a minute and then begins to dress. Natasha wonders if he is married, has children; she wonders why he never asks her about herself. Her other regulars probe her constantly, fancy themselves white knights destined to rescue her from the profane life. Uncle Blue does not care about Natasha's whereabouts when he is absent; he does not care what led her to this profession, whether she cries at night, whether she longs for a calm suburban marriage. A single problem lies knotted in his mind; all his thoughts are directed at unraveling its complexities. Any errors will lead to trouble, and Uncle Blue has worked too hard, for too long, to tolerate self-inflicted trouble. The stupidities and betrayals of other people can never be eliminated; that is the essential problem facing every great businessman. In the slop of this world, a realist seeks only to minimize damage. Tonight Uncle Blue will murder a man. He cannot afford to make any mistakes.

SIX

JAKOB IS ONE of the greatest pedestrians in New York's history. He angles through the crowd, slipping the jabs and hooks of on-coming walkers, ducking below tree branches, tiptoeing along the curb's edge, dodging the scattered piles of dog shit, waiting for an opening, and then darting into the clear. Like all good citizens of the city, Jakob has learned to avert his eyes from the freaks of the street: the panhandling amputees, the palsied church-step dwellers, the deranged sideshows picking through the garbage. .

He threads his way through the rushing mob outside the 72nd Street subway station. Past the turnstile, down the stairs, he finds the emptiest stretch of platform; when the train arrives he burrows into the scrum of the packed car, snatches a strap, and holds on as the train accelerates. Jakob's tolerance for alcohol is minimal. The two beers he drank with LoBianco have left him disoriented, a woozy wedge driven between mind and body. He pictures him-self, his true *self*, commanding this spastic Jakob android from a re-mote location. What is this body? he wonders. And why did I have to get it?

Sometimes when he wakes up in the morning the face he sees in the bathroom mirror seems unfamiliar and unhelpful. He will squint at this tired face like a man at a high school reunion trying to remember the name of a classmate vaguely associated with disappointing times. Jakob doesn't like the body he's got, but it's more than that; he feels he doesn't truly belong to this body. There was a mistake back in the beginning; his brain was loaded into the wrong skull; the proper Jakob body sits naked and inert in a corner somewhere or else dances at the command of a usurper mind.

He brims his Yankees cap low, reads the advertisements posted above the seats. One is a cartoon strip, an ongoing AIDS-awareness saga about a group of New Yorkers. This particular strip is in Spanish, which Jakob does not read, but he sees that the heroes are in a cemetery, apparently for the funeral of their friend Rafael. Silver tears drip from one woman's eyes. Jakob notices that someone has drawn fat nipples onto her blouse, and he frowns at the impropriety.

The train stops at Columbus Circle and Jakob remembers what he always remembers in this station, the time nine years ago when Monty, on a dare, leapt from the subway platform onto the tracks, skipped over the third rail, hoisted himself onto the opposite platform, kissed a pretty girl on the cheek, and returned, grinning—not at his own audacity, which he took for granted, but at the girl's open-mouthed shock. Jakob never understood where Montgomery came from, what produced such wildness, such an absolute disdain for the consequences.

Jakob wonders what a seventeen-year-old Monty would have made of Mary D'Annunzio. Not much, probably. The boys in her grade don't seem to fancy her. She is flat-chested, rough-voiced, unwashed; she sits through class silent and scowling, unless she launches one of her diatribes, which are generally cranky and always unrelated to the topic at hand. Her friends are all seniors, "that androgynous crew of dope fiends," in LoBianco's phrase, who seem to be forever clustered in the school's cafeteria, drinking coffee, their rumpled black clothes foul with cigarette smoke, their hands marked with blurred door stamps from last night's round of clubbing. Jakob doesn't know whether any of these young hipsters are coupled off. He suspects that one lean David Bowie look-alike might be intimate with Mary; they're often engaged in head-to-head low-voiced debates that leave Jakob sick with loneliness. Jakob saw this entire gang one time in the Sheep Meadow, sprawled in a circle around an older Rastafarian who played Scratch Perry songs on an acoustic guitar. Nobody noticed Jakob and he hurried past, not studying Mary's bare belly, hardly aware of her fingertip tracing the rim of her navel.

I don't want to be a teacher, thinks Jakob glumly, watching the passengers shove their way out of the subway car. I want to be an old Rastafarian. Jesus, Fourteenth Street! He slips through the doors a moment before they close and follows the herd through the turnstiles and up the stairs.

Outside the air has grown markedly colder in the fifteen minutes since he ventured belowground; the chill helps him regain sobriety. By the time he gets to Slattery's building the first snow has begun to fall, heavy flakes tumbling slowly by streetlight and melting on the sidewalk. It will never stick, thinks Jakob, disappointed as a schoolboy.

He announces himself to a doorman sitting behind a marble-topped desk, a thin-lipped, red-haired kid, face awash in freckles, who wears an oversized epauletted uniform. The doorman picks up the intercom phone and buzzes Slattery's apartment.

"Jakob's here," he says; then, "I don't know, let me ask." He looks up at Jakob. "Jakob who?"

"Ha-ha. Tell him ha-ha."

The doorman grins and speaks into the phone. "You hear that? Okay, you got it." He hangs up and points at the elevator. "Fifth floor."

"I know."

An old lady, bent and wretched, stands in a corner of the mirrored lobby, staring down at a potted Chinese rubber plant. A nurse waits by her side. Jakob walks quickly to the elevator and pushes the button.

"Come on, Charlotte," says the nurse, in a singsong Caribbean accent. She catches Jakob stealing a backward glance and winks at him. "Come on, girl."

"I have to sit down," wails Charlotte.

"We're in the lobby. Come on. Into the apartment and then you sit down. Then you sit down for hours. Let's go."

Jakob stifles a sneeze and the old woman turns her head. "Louis?" she calls out, peering across the lobby. "Louis?"

I am not Louis, thinks Jakob, scrounging in his back pocket for a tissue. Charlotte slumps against the wall and sinks down to the floor, bird legs splayed before her. "I can't go any farther. Where's Louis?"

"That's not Louis," the nurse tells her, smiling at Jakob.

Jakob never wants to grow old, never wants to be like Charlotte, humpbacked and helpless, collapsed in the corner of a mirrored lobby.

"Can I help?" he finally asks, terrified that the nurse will say yes.

"You're sweet," says the nurse. Jakob interprets that as a no. The electric floor indicator above the elevator shines an unchanging 4. He tugs on the brim of his Yankees cap.

"I told you she was no good," says Charlotte. "I told you, Louis."

"That's not Louis," says the nurse. "That's not your son. Come on now, get up, girl, we'll miss your shows."

Jakob pushes the button two more times. He usually rolls his eyes at people who keep pushing the elevator button, trying to goad a lazy machine into action, as if the elevator could be harassed into service like a recalcitrant waiter: *All right, all right, the ketchup, I'm coming.* He jabs the button again with his knuckle.

"I warned you," mutters Charlotte.

At last the car arrives and Jakob enters. He is facing Charlotte now; he can't avoid seeing her head bowed down to her chest, her entire shrunken body convulsed with shudders. "Evie!" she cries out. "Evie!"

"Hush, girl, I'm right here. Come on, give me your hand."

Jakob passes his fingers over the electric eye and the closing doors jerk open. "Hi, sorry, are you sure you're okay there?"

Evie looks at him over her shoulder. "Sure we're sure. We do this every night."

"Louis?"

For a second Jakob wishes he *were* Louis, wishes he could say *I'm here, Mom*, then cross the lobby and lift the old woman to her feet. That would be heroic. The elevator doors slide shut and Jakob closes his eyes. Between the walls of the building he rises. He imagines himself a bucket of water being cranked to the top of the well. It hits him now how tired he is; he has not slept soundly in weeks. And Monty? Can Monty sleep at all?

Slattery's trophy apartment, a sprawl of largely empty rooms, strikes Jakob as the perfect example of a type: the Young Man with Money without Woman apartment. The television set in the living room is so gigantic that the weatherman frightens Jakob. Slattery mistakes his friend's disturbed look. "Big, huh?"

"Yes, it's very big. When did you get it?"

"Couple of weeks ago. Gave myself a little gift. I mean, I've got to start spending the money sometime."

What a vulgar expression, thinks Jakob. *The money*. Vulgar in large part, Jakob would admit, because his friend's annual earnings are approximately twenty-three point seven times greater than his own, an approximation Jakob figured on his calculator one afternoon when he was supposed to be calculating grade point averages for his freshmen.

They sit on a yellow sofa that Slattery slept on for two years as a child, before the family moved to a bigger place in Bay Ridge. Jakob wonders why Slattery doesn't spend a little more of *the money* on new furniture. The living room, larger than Jakob's entire apartment, is empty save for the old sofa, the mammoth television, and a stack of artificial logs by the fireplace. Slattery's bottle of beer rests on the hardwood floor between his feet. A large rug, rolled and corded, lies under the windows. Propped up in the corner is a glossy red electric guitar, another of Slattery's gifts to himself.

The back of the sofa bears twin dark smudges from thousands of hours supporting dirty heads; Jakob's side sags because of a spring that snapped when the teenage Slattery held his younger brother facedown on the cushions and then jumped on his back, sending the boy to the hospital with a chipped vertebra. Jakob pities Eoin—the kid still seems shell-shocked, as if his childhood were a war he barely survived.

The television is flanked by twin speaker towers. Smaller speakers hang from the ceiling, providing surround sound, which Jakob imagines is wonderful for movies. For the weatherman, though, it's agitating: the professionally cheerful voice comes at Jakob from every possible angle. "We might be looking at our first major winter storm for the New York metropolitan area, and I'll tell you what, Carol, it could be a doozy. Expect anywhere from four to ten inches of snow—"

"Ten inches of snow!" shouts Slattery. "We ought to drive upstate day after tomorrow, do some skiing. I just bought some Völkls—racing skis."

"I don't know how to ski," says Jakob.

"So what, neither do I. But ten inches of snow. . . . Maybe not this weekend."

The weatherman's voice echoes in the underfurnished room.

Jakob shudders. "Do you think real human beings use the word *doozy*?"

"What?"

"Have you taken any lessons yet?" asks Jakob, pointing at the red guitar.

Slattery shakes his head. "You think I have time for guitar lessons? It's pretty nice, though, isn't it?"

"It's really nice," says Jakob.

"Yeah. That's a nice color red."

"Do you want another beer?" asks Jakob, anxious to get away from the giant newscasters.

"Yeah, thanks."

The kitchen is suspiciously clean. Jakob examines the shimmering stainless steel sink, runs his finger along the countertop, finds no sticky spots, no crumbs. The enormous black stove, complete with six burners and an integrated griddle free of splatters and fingerprints, has apparently never been sullied by the tawdry chore of cooking. Bastard has a maid coming in, Jakob decides. The Sub-Zero refrigerator is well stocked, crammed with bottled olives, horseradish mustard, a round of smoked mozzarella wrapped in plastic, a roasted turkey drumstick in aluminum foil. This looks like my parents' refrigerator, thinks Jakob, sadly.

"There's no beer in here!" yells Jakob, louder than he meant. The echo of his own voice in the kitchen sounds bitter.

"Hold on a second."

Jakob returns to the living room, watches Slattery watching the national news. "There's no beer in the refrigerator."

"Did you really look?"

"No, I didn't *really* look. Was I supposed to *really* look?"

"Have you seen this?" asks Slattery. "Here, sit down, watch this."

Jakob sits reluctantly, trying not to stare directly at the screen.

"This elephant in Bangkok got loose in the streets, last night or something. Look at this."

Someone with a handheld video camera recorded the scene, a gray elephant stomping down the middle of a broad thoroughfare, followed by a cheering crowd of men, women, and children. Police officers try to hold the people back, setting up orange sawhorses and waving their billy clubs, but everyone ignores the officers in the happy pandemonium. Soldiers in military fatigues track the elephant through the scopes of their high-powered rifles.

"I was watching this on CNN an hour ago," says Slattery. "They said old elephants lose their minds sometimes, just snap. Watch this."

Black quills appear on the elephant's weathered hide and Jakob listens to the reporter describing the tranquilizer darts, six in all, each loaded with enough sedative to knock out any reasonable elephant. The beast shudders for a moment, shaking its massive head, the great ears flopping back and forth. Then it turns in its tracks and charges toward the sidewalk. The crowd gathered there disperses in all directions, like billiard balls after a good break. The elephant lowers its head and smashes through the glass storefront of what appears to be an electronics shop.

"Goddamn," says Slattery, rocking back and forth on the sofa. "Look at that mother go!"

The soldiers begin firing their rifles—loud, echoing retorts—and the video image shakes before being replaced on screen by a Thai military spokesman standing behind a lectern, explaining the day's events.

"They killed it?" asks Jakob.

"Oh, yes," says Slattery, "they did indeed. Poor fuck went for a walk in the wrong part of town."

Jakob wonders what caused the animal to snap: old age, faulty synapses in the brain, the long-resisted urge to take an afternoon stroll down the avenue? He tugs the bill of his Yankees cap lower on his forehead.

"What time is Monty coming over?"

"He's not. He's eating with his dad. We're going to meet him later on."

How can Monty eat? Jakob wonders. How can he swallow his food?

The television screen goes black for a moment between commercials, and Jakob sees his face reflected in the glass. "Do you think I look like a ferret?"

"A ferret?" Slattery laughs. "That's good, I hadn't thought of that before."

"So do I?"

"One of the kids in your class told you that?"

Jakob frowns. "Nobody told me. I was just wondering."

"Somebody must have said something. You wouldn't just think, all of a sudden, Hey, I look like a ferret. You've been looking at your face for twenty-six years."

"Actually," says Jakob, "let's drop it."

"I don't even know what a ferret looks like. But yeah, you might resemble one."

"Fine, thanks. You're a wonderful human being."

Slattery pats Jakob on the head. "And you're not bad for a ferret. I'm going to take a crap and then we can go eat." He lifts himself from the sofa with a groan. He squats low to the ground for a
moment and then straightens up, left knee creaking loudly.
"Christ," he says, limping to the bathroom.

Jakob sits alone with the television, staring sullenly at the
square-jawed anchorman, angry without knowing the exact cause
of his anger. Sometimes he is fairly sure that he doesn't like Slattery, that he never liked him, even if Slattery is his best friend.
Jakob remembers the first day of ninth grade, walking through the
school gates, uneager to spend another year with the tanned boys
who milled in the courtyard wearing loosely knotted ties and boat
shoes. When he met Frank and Monty he thrilled at their Brooklyn accents, their carefully combed hair the opposite of traditional
prep school dishevelment. Both of them had been in scores of fistfights, which mesmerized Jakob, who had been in exactly zero. But
they were out of their element here, nervous around the diffident
poise of the old-timers, intimidated by the casual displays of
wealth. They immediately fastened upon Jakob as a sympathetic
figure who knew his way around. During the convocation that
opened the school year, Monty nudged Jakob with his elbow and
motioned to an older boy sitting several pews in front of them.
"That's a Ralph Lauren jacket the guy's wearing. Thing costs four
hundred bucks." Jakob was delighted by the immediate intimacy,
by the presumption that they came from similar backgrounds and
that both of them would be shocked by a high school junior wearing a four-hundred-dollar jacket. Three months went by before
Jakob had his two new friends over to his apartment. He feared
they would lump him with the rest of the soft aristocrats in their
grade. But by the time Monty and Frank showed up at the Elinsky household, they had already been to parties at triplexes on Fifth
Avenue, townhouses on Park, a spectacular beach cottage in the
Hamptons—and Jakob's place, though perfectly nice, was far from
intimidating.

The other old-timers in the class at first affected disdain for the newcomers, the "F.A.s," students receiving Financial Assistance, two Irish, two Puerto Rican, and four black, shipped in from Brooklyn, Queens, and the Bronx. Lords of the Outer Boroughs was the initial review, a moniker that Monty seized for his own and ran through his hip-hop spell checker; the Outta Buro Lordz soon became the most admired clique in the school. Jakob reveled in his status as an honorary member, if always conscious that he lived, after all, on Central Park West, that his father was a tax attorney, that his knowledge of the outer boroughs consisted of Yankee Stadium to the north and Kennedy, LaGuardia, and his cousins in Forest Hills to the east.

Now it is Slattery and his associates who dine at expensive restaurants, while Jakob grades grammar quizzes in his eleven-foot-square apartment, boiling water for another meal of spaghetti and tomato paste. Jakob generally enjoys playing this game, the How Pathetic Is Your Life? game, but not now, not tonight, not when his friend is headed for federal prison in the morning.

Slattery finally emerges from the bathroom, drying his hands on a towel. "You ready? I'm starving."

Jakob turns off the television with the remote control and stands. "What's he going to do with Doyle?"

"Huh?"

"Where's Doyle going to end up?"

"Oh. I don't know." Slattery throws the towel onto the coffee table, opens a closet, and pulls a black cashmere overcoat off a wooden hanger. "With Nat?"

Jakob shakes his head. "I doubt it."

"With his dad? I really don't know. You like this coat? A friend of mine brought it back from London."

"Frank," says Jakob, picking at his fingernails, "are you ready for this?"

"Ready for what?"

"For tonight?"

"I got to tell you," says Slattery, buttoning the coat, "it was such a crazy day at work, I haven't even thought about it much."

"You haven't?" asks Jakob, startled. "He's your best friend."

"You don't have to explain it to me, I understand that. What do you want me to do? We're going out with him, we'll have a few drinks, what am I going to do? Come on, let's move. Tie your shoes."

Jakob gets down on one knee and begins lacing his rubber-soled hiking boots. "I'm nervous about seeing him. I really am; I'm scared. It's like visiting a friend who's in the hospital with cancer. What do you say? He's going to be living in a cell for seven years. What do you say to him?"

Slattery shrugs. "You know what? I don't think you say anything. I think we go out with him tonight, and we try to have a good time, and if he wants to talk about it, we talk about it. He's going to hell for seven years—what am I going to do, wish him luck? We get him drunk and try to give him one more good night."

Jakob ties a double knot and stands. "You make it sound like you've done this before."

"I have. My cousin got sent up for three years. Ready?" Slattery opens the front door and waits for Jakob, one hand on the light switch.

"He did? You never told me that. What for?"

"He's a fucking thief, that's what for."

The biggest scandal in Jakob's family was a bulimic cousin. He wonders what other secrets Slattery has been keeping. "So he got through it okay? In prison and all?"

"No. Not even close to okay. Come on, come on, let's go."

"Wait a second," says Jakob, patting his hip pockets. "Where's my wallet?"

"Oh, Jesus."

"I had it when I came in here. I know I had it."

"It's sitting on the sofa, schmuck."

Jakob retrieves the wallet and pockets it. "It's weird, though, I think, just knowing Monty, I think he'll be okay." He sees the expression on Slattery's face and continues, hurriedly, "No, no, I'm not saying it will be easy. If it was me, I'd never make it a day, I know that. But it's Monty. He's tough. He's always been tough."

"No, he hasn't," says Slattery, flicking off the lights, "and he won't be okay. I don't know what you're thinking, Jake. There's not going to be a happy ending."

Jakob exits the apartment and waits while Slattery locks the door. "I'm not saying *happy*. I'm just saying—"

"You don't know what the fuck you're talking about. Tough? How do you know from tough? What do you think, because he wins a couple fights at Campbell-Sawyer, that means he's a tough guy in Otisville? You don't understand the trouble he's in. You don't get it. Monty's got three choices, and none of them are good." They walk down the blue-carpeted hallway, Slattery twirling his key chain.

"Three choices," says Jakob, impatient. Slattery always talks to him as if he were a dense child, not quick enough to understand the world's complexities.

"Okay. One, he can run. Get on a bus going to wherever and just hope they never catch up with him. That's number one."

"He won't do that. His dad's bar—"

"I'm not saying what he *will* do. I'm saying what his choices are. Number two—" Slattery makes a gun with his thumb and index finger and points it at his temple.

Jakob's eyes go wide. "Kill himself? Not a chance. So what's the third option?"

"The third option?" Slattery thinks for a moment. "Oh, the third option is he goes to prison."

Jakob nods. "That's what's going to happen. He'll go, and he'll make it through."

"Okay. Maybe. But no matter what, it's bye-bye Monty."

"What does that mean?"

Slattery raises his thumb. "If he runs, he's gone. You'll never see him again." He raises his index finger, the top joint crooked from wrestling days. "If he pulls the trigger, he's gone. They'll keep the

casket closed." He raises his middle finger. "If they lock him away,
he's gone. You'll never see him again."

"I'll see him again," says Jakob. "I'll see him when he gets out."

The elevator doors open and Slattery steps inside. "I wouldn't
bet on it. You think you're still going to be friends? You think
you'll kick back with a couple beers and reminisce? Forget it, Jake.
It's over after tonight. You getting in?"

SEVEN

W"HAT'S GOOD HERE?" asks Monty, reading the menu from a blackboard on the wall.

"The veal," says his father. "The veal's good. That's what I usually get."

"Okay." Monty leans back in his chair and surveys the restaurant: a low-ceilinged relic just north of Houston Street, one of the last of the old-school Italians, where they still serve spaghetti and meatballs, eggplant parmesan, chicken cacciatore.

"Taking off Thursday night," says Monty. "That's big of you. Who's minding the place?"

"Kennelly's taking care of it."

"Kennelly? He's going to drink all your rum. You trust Kennelly?"

"It's only a couple hours. You said you were meeting your friends, so I figured ten o'clock—"

"That's fine," says Monty. He plays with the label on their bottle of red wine. The waitress, an old woman with a face like a crumpled paper bag, takes their order. She wears a platinum-blond wig and false eyelashes; she beams when she hears Monty's selection.

"Good pick," she says, her front teeth red with lipstick. "Veal's the best thing here." She shuffles away and Monty thinks, *She'll be dead before I get back here.*

"So I talked to Sal—"

"Ah, come on, Dad."

"See if he can help with anything."

"Dad, come on, what are you thinking? Sal? The guy's been out of the picture for twenty years."

"He might know some people in there."

"The guy's about a hundred years old. He sits around playing gin rummy all day. What's Sal going to do for me?"

"He still knows people. He could put in—"

"Dad, would you please? I'll be all right. Just, please, don't get involved in this. Okay?"

"You're still going to be a young man when you get out. I know," says Mr. Brogan, raising his hands, for Monty is shaking his head. "I know you don't think so. But listen to me. You keep your head down in there. Don't start any trouble—"

"Enough." Monty stares at the backs of his hands. He wills them to quit trembling, but they won't.

When the waitress brings out their food, Mr. Brogan diligently cuts the spinach leaves on his plate into smaller and smaller squares. He had wanted desperately to give his son something, to encourage him in some way, but now, watching the boy try to eat, he knows it is useless. How do you say, *It's only seven years*? Mr. Brogan's father was a barman; Mr. Brogan grew up in bars and worked in them his whole life, sometimes rough places where a wrong word could lead to a beating or worse. But he understands that nothing in his experience can come close to what waits for Monty, that Monty is traveling to a foreign land Mr. Brogan knows only from rumor.

Mr. Brogan's bar is his bond to the court, his guarantee that Monty will not run away. Since June, Monty has been free because of the bar: free before trial, during trial, after conviction, after sentencing. Mr. Brogan has owned the bar for thirty years, but sometimes he wishes Monty would run. Let them have the place; let them try to make money off it. Caught between Bensonhurst and Bay Ridge, he owns a neighborhood bar without a neighborhood. Most of his patrons work at the hospital down the block or in the stores on 86th Street; they stop off for a drink before driving home. They are loyal, his customers, they like him and confide in him, but they do not have much money to spend.

"This should never have happened," says Mr. Brogan, staring at his glass of soda water.

"All right, let's not start now. It's a little late in the game."

"I know," says Mr. Brogan. "I know it, and I'm sorry, Monty. I should never have let you get involved."

Monty raps the tabletop with his knuckles. "Hey. Let it go. You had nothing to do with it, okay? Don't start with this now."

"I just wish we could have talked about it. You could have made so much money in a *real* business; you didn't need that . . . You should never have gotten involved with that."

But money was never the sole draw for Monty. He hadn't grown up poor and he wasn't greedy; he liked fast cars and Italian shoes but he didn't need them, didn't hunger for them. It was more about sway. Sway helps make your money and money helps make your sway, but sway is not money. Sway is walking into a clothes shop and knowing you can buy anything on the shelves, true, but sway is also the clerk opening the shop after hours so you can walk through the aisles alone with your girlfriend; sway is the clerk unlocking the back room to show you the latest deliveries, still sheathed in plastic bags; sway is the clerk standing silent in the corner while you browse, and the clerk won't complain if you paw the merchandise and kiss your girl for an hour because he knows about you and the trouble's not worth it. Sway is making a phone call in the morning and having courtside seats at Madison Square Garden that night. Sway is entering a nightclub through the staff entrance so you can skip the metal detector. Sway is locking eyes with an undercover cop on the subway; you know what he is and he knows what you are, and you wink at him because he drives a battered Buick and you drive a Corvette, and he cannot touch you.

The Corvette is gone now. The government took title after Monty's indictment. He wonders where it is—parked in some smirking suburbanite's driveway or else still waiting in a federal lot for auction day. Monty does not love cars the way some men do, but he was proud of his vehicle, proud of its low-slung black body, the roar of its engine, the way he could make it bolt through the gaps in midtown traffic. On lucky days he'd find a string of green lights and cruise home in style.

In thirteen hours, home becomes the Otisville Federal Correctional Institution; a Catskill Eagle bus will take him there. They will give him the proper documents to sign, they will strip-search him, and they will fingerprint him—again.

Monty doesn't mention Otisville or the Corvette or the principle of sway to his father. Instead, he says, "I didn't hear you complaining when you were borrowing money. Not a word back then."

"No. You're right. That was a mistake."

Mr. Brogan remembers when Monty was an infant, red-skinned and kicking. The boy would squeeze his eyes shut and pound on the blue blanket he lay on, wailing weakly—short, stuttered cries—in the months before his lungs were strong enough for true volume. His mother would pick him up from the crib, one hand supporting his head; she would walk with him and sing to him. She could never hold a tune but Monty did not seem to mind; he watched her obsessively, his green eyes locked on her green eyes. Or she would read to him from a picture book while his fuzzed head rested on her breast. She would read to him and he would listen quietly, long before he knew what the words meant: *Goodnight stars, goodnight air, goodnight noises everywhere.* And Mr. Brogan would stand in doorways, always a little apart. Not jealous exactly, but maybe a little jealous, always conscious that this was an alliance to which he could only be witness.

There was something fierce about the boy's love for his mother and her love for him. They were a beautiful pair. Later, when they marched down the street together, his hand clutching hers, people turned to watch them, smiling. *What a darling boy.* She had insisted on naming her son after Montgomery Clift, her favorite actor, and she got her wish over her husband's objections. Back then Mr. Brogan felt uneasy about the name; he thought it was bad luck to name their only child after a fallen movie star. But Montgomery it was, and Mr. Brogan was glad to see that the boy looked like his mother: the same rich black hair; the same small, even teeth; the same straight nose; the same eyes, so green as to be unsettling. He was a beautiful boy and he grew into a beautiful man, and Mr. Brogan was always proud to have such a handsome son. Now, though, he wishes Monty were a little less handsome.

"I've got to get going, Dad. I'm meeting the boys in a few minutes." The veal chop sits half eaten on Monty's plate.

"I'll be there tomorrow," says Mr. Brogan. He removes his wallet from the inside pocket of his jacket.

"Tomorrow? What for? I get on a bus and I'm gone."

"Forget the bus. I'll drive you. It'll take half as long."

Monty frowns, wiping his mouth with his napkin and backing his chair away from the table: "No, thanks, Dad. I'd rather say goodbye here."

Mr. Brogan pulls a small photograph from his wallet and hands it to his son. "Take this. They'll let you keep it."

Monty holds the picture carefully in his fingers. The three of them, the whole family, stand before a lavishly decorated tree. On the back, written in pencil: *Christmas Eve, 1976.* Monty at six, wearing yellow Mighty Mouse pajamas, holding his mother's hand and staring at the floor. Mr. Brogan remembers how they had pleaded with the boy to smile, had joked and coaxed and threatened, all to no avail.

Mr. Brogan tells the story and Monty nods, though he doesn't remember any of it. But it hurts him to see how lovely she was, how young. Because he cannot remember her that way; he cannot remember her beautiful, only wasted and crooked on the hospital bed.

Mr. Brogan clears his throat. "She—"

"Don't, Dad," says Monty, still looking at her face. "Not now."

Monty carefully inserts the photograph in his own wallet, lays down money for the check, stands, kisses his father on the forehead, and walks out of the restaurant. Mr. Brogan closes his eyes and listens to his own breathing. He has one wife and she's buried in Woodlawn; he has one son and he's headed for Otisville.

EIGHT

A FACELESS MAN knocks on the door in Naturelle's dream, but the sound is all wrong, the knocks too high-pitched, and she realizes in the seconds before waking that what she hears are Doyle's claws clattering on the hardwood floor. A rough tongue begins licking her face and she opens her eyes.

"Hey. Hey."

Doyle's front paws are planted firmly on the mattress, brown eyes unblinking in his blunted face.

"Come on, Doyle, get down. Down. Down, Doyle, get down."

He licks her face again and she tries to shove him away, but Doyle thinks she is playing and bows his head to lick her wrist. Naturelle sits up and checks the digital clock on the nightstand: 9:23. For a second she believes that morning has come, that Montgomery is gone, that she has missed everything. But outside the city is dark, as dark as the city can get. The night is waiting. And what bothers her most is the feeling that slid through her when she thought it was morning—not panic or disappointment or sadness, but relief.

Doyle barks sharply and Naturelle stares at him guiltily, as if the dog has been reading her thoughts. "What?" she asks him. But he just watches her, wagging the stump of his tail.

"Now?" She rises from the bed and walks to the window, looks out at the fat flakes of snow dropping slowly to the street. Several inches already blanket the parked cars. "It's snowing," she tells the dog. "I don't know, Doyle. It's really coming down."

Doyle barks again, now standing by the closet, and Naturelle raises her hands in surrender. "All right, all right." She bends down to touch her toes and then opens the closet door and begins rummaging for her running clothes. When she steps into her tights, Doyle sprints into the living room; Naturelle hears his claws skidding on the floor, his excited breathing, his muscular little body banging into furniture.

Ten minutes later they are jogging counterclockwise around the Central Park reservoir. The snow is falling thickly; the track is only visible for ten yards in either direction. Beyond the chain-link fence to her left is nothing but white, same for the woods to the right, a fringe of bushes and trees hedging the unknown. Naturelle wears a hooded jacket and heavy mittens. She has released Doyle's leash and the dog runs free, now twenty feet ahead, sniffing at a clump of frozen shit, now thirty feet back, chasing a terrified squirrel through the underbrush. Naturelle knows that Montgomery would be furious if he saw his dog unleashed. "Give the city an excuse and they'll fry a pit bull in butter," he likes to say, but it's too exhausting running *and* controlling the dog. Doyle is too strong for his own good.

She has asked Montgomery a dozen times what he plans to do with the dog, and she has never got a straight answer. Where will Doyle go? After February, which Monty already paid for, Naturelle will have to move out of their apartment, back to the Bronx with her mother for a while, until she can find a job and get a place of her own. And Mrs. Rosario would never allow Doyle—or anything else that belonged to Montgomery Brogan—into her home. Doyle and Mrs. Rosario met one time and hated each other: the dog, ears flattened against his skull, had snarled at her on first smell; the woman, scowling, had said, "Looks like he been chewed on by rats." And Montgomery, to make everything worse, had pointed at Mrs. Rosario's dyed hair and said, "It's probably the hair. He hates anything that shade of red."

Naturelle's mother had warned her about Monty, and now that she has been proven correct she wastes no opportunity to gloat. What angers Naturelle most is that her mother seems happy about the whole situation, glad that the moody white boy turned out to be the criminal she suspected. "I don't know why you stay there," Mrs. Rosario says. "Somebody going to come shoot that boy in the head, and shoot you too if you in the way." What makes her mother's comments doubly irritating is that Naturelle has had the same thought, lying awake in the dark.

She has always known that one day Monty would be arrested or murdered, that he would leave their bed in the morning and not return at night. She could not imagine growing old with him— she could not imagine Monty growing old at all. In her mind she tried to gray his hair, to furrow his skin with wrinkles and put a hitch in his loose stride, but the pictured Monty always shucked off these disguises and grinned at her, free and easy and relentlessly young. He was like a smart boy who has not yet learned to fake an interest in other people. He was careless with the affections of his family and friends. He had always been loved; he never had to work for love.

So why does she stay? Often when Naturelle pictures Monty she pictures him driving, his left hand curled around the underside of the steering wheel. She remembers one time, riding with him down Second Avenue, when every light turned green at the perfect moment and they sped happily along, the fingertips of Monty's right hand tapping the inside of her thigh in time to the music on the radio. Then, on 12th Street, a yellow cab shot through a red light and Naturelle knew they had no time to brake; she saw what was going to happen, saw their Corvette broadside the taxi, saw their hood accordion and their bodies slam forward, saw it all in an instant—except it didn't happen. Monty accelerated and cut behind the cab, just missing its rear bumper. His fingertips never skipped a beat.

Thirty seconds later, when she was able to speak, she said, "I thought we were going to die."

"The cab? I saw him coming." A commercial came on the air and Monty switched stations, searching until he found a song he liked.

And that was why she loved him, because at his best he possessed more natural grace than any other man she ever met, because some days he performed miracles and didn't even notice.

There were nights, before all the troubles began, when Naturelle could not imagine wanting to be with anyone else. She felt important walking around with Monty. People watched them, bent their heads together, and whispered when they entered restaurants. The bouncers at most of the nightclubs in Manhattan knew Monty; they would see him approaching and nod, drape their huge arms around his shoulders, and huddle for a minute's quiet conversation. Even when Monty did not know the bruiser working the door, he would march with Naturelle to the front of the line, announce, "I'm Montgomery Brogan," and usher her inside. Nobody ever stopped him and he never, ever, paid a cover charge. Naturelle imagined some of these bouncers probably recognized his name and knew that he always gave a generous cut to security. But other times she was sure the name itself meant nothing, it was just the way he said it: "I'm Montgomery Brogan." He knew he was getting in, and the bouncers sensed this and never stopped him.

Naturelle hears the footfalls of another jogger approaching from behind. She glances over her shoulder: a lone man, wearing a polyurethane track suit and a ski cap. Doyle? thinks Naturelle. Where you at, boy?

"Another fanatic, huh?" says the man, slowing his pace to jog alongside her. Naturelle nods but says nothing. "I thought . . . I'd be the only one out here. How many laps you running?"

"Three," she says, scouting the bushes for the black dog.

"You run a good pace. You were on . . . your school's track team, huh?"

"No," says Naturelle, who lettered all four years in the distance events.

"We've got this corporate challenge . . . coming up in March."

He is puffing mightily as he runs, his words interrupted by great steamy snorts and exhalations. "You know . . . ten kilometers for charity . . . that whole deal. My bank gives a lot of money . . . but only if . . . only if . . . I finish the race."

"Good luck." Naturelle is trying to decide whether to speed up or slow down.

"I work down at Shreve, Zimmer . . . investment bank."

Deciding that the man is about to collapse, Naturelle speeds up. "I have a friend who works there."

"Yeah? Whew . . . who's that?"

"Frank Slattery. You know him?"

"I've heard some stories about *that* guy . . . I'm dying . . . okay, yeah . . . Frank Slattery."

"What kind of stories?"

"Jesus, slow down. . . . He a good friend of yours?"

She thinks about it. "I guess so."

The man coughs into the back of his hand. "This is *serious* snow, huh?"

"What kind of stories?"

"You can really run. Man . . . oh, man . . . I don't know him real well, but . . . slow down, slow down . . . whew . . . supposed to be . . . real ballbuster."

"Yeah?"

"Serious hard-ass. Word is . . . goddamn me . . . word is he almost got canned today."

"Really?"

"Nah . . . that won't happen. He's a star. Christ, lady . . . you're killing me."

Doyle jumps out of the snowy nothingness, barking madly, his fangs glittering in the lamplight.

"*Whoa!* Fuck me, whoa, whoa, whoa!" The banker jumps for the chain-link fence and climbs midway up as Doyle growls below, gnashing his teeth.

"Hey!" yells Naturelle. "Doyle! Hey! Come over here! Doyle! Come! Here!" Doyle finally obeys, trotting over to Naturelle's side.

"Safe?" asks the banker.

"I'm really sorry. He gets a little hyper."

"Hyper? That's what you call it?"

The banker drops from the fence and stands doubled over, his hands on his hips, gasping for air. Naturelle jogs in place, hoping he's not about to have a heart attack. "You okay?"

"That thing . . . oh, Jesus . . . that thing is yours?"

"He's my boyfriend's."

"He's . . ." The man begins to laugh, still bent over the track. "I've got some luck . . . huh? The one woman I've met . . . outside the office in the last month, and she's . . . got a boyfriend *and* a pit bull. Oh, God. Okay . . . I'm okay. A boyfriend *and* a pit bull. Plus, I can't even keep up with her!" He laughs again, looking up at Naturelle and shaking his head. "Sorry. I don't get out much. They've got us locked in there one hundred hours a week."

"Sorry about Doyle," says Naturelle, turning from the man and continuing her jog.

"Hey!" he calls after her. Naturelle pivots, running backward while watching the man.

"Are you Italian?" he asks.

Naturelle shakes her head. "Puerto Rican."

"Oh. Okay." He thinks for a moment. "But you're Catholic, right?"

"Uh-huh." Naturelle is now fifteen yards away, Doyle by her side. The banker is disappearing in the snow.

"What's your name?"

"Maria."

"Wish me luck in the race, Maria!" he calls after her. "That I don't die or something."

"Good luck!" she yells and faces front again. "And you," she says, looking down at Doyle, "are a bad dog. You leave me like that again and I'll kick your little black ass."

They run on through the snow, Naturelle breathing easily, her small feet beating a steady rhythm. Two years ago she ran the marathon. A beautiful day. Half the city turned out to watch her and her comrades run the five boroughs, everyone cheering for a common cause. It wasn't a competition, that was the beauty of it. Nobody outside the professionals really cared what place they came in; finishing was the point. Coming across the Verrazano in a herd of thousands, Naturelle had felt, for the first time in her life, that she truly belonged to this city.

In the final miles of the race, crossing 86th Street in Manhattan, she looked for Monty, who had promised to be there. No Monty. She searched the crowd for his pale face but could not find him. And as she ran she realized that he really didn't give a shit. She had trained for five months, run sixty miles a week, and established a new diet limiting her fat and sugar intake—that was the worst part. Naturelle inherited her sweet tooth from her grandfather, who came to the Bronx as a young boy and still worked as an orderly at Mount Sinai Hospital. At least three times a day she needed her fix: black licorice, white chocolate, gummy coke bottles, peanut butter ice cream, macadamia nut cookies, coconut haystacks, truffles, candied orange peel, halvah—anything good. For five months she went without her beloved sweets, five months of the spartan life, making do with plums, figs, nectarines, and, especially, bananas. Naturelle would always sigh when she unpeeled a banana. How could anyone get excited for a banana? But she did it, she had put in the work and on the day of the marathon she was coming through, her form perfect, her wind good, her legs holding up nicely. While the man she lived with, the man who claimed to love her, slept on in their king-size bed or spoke quietly into his cell phone or watched cartoon cats and mice chase each other through yellow houses.

She was furious at him until 81st Street, when she heard him calling her name and looked back to see him chasing after her.

"Christ, didn't you hear me calling? How many fucking Naturelles are there?"

A clutch of onlookers standing nearby began laughing, and Monty stared at them and then smiled himself. He wore a white

T-shirt and jeans; he looked like he was still in high school. They jogged shoulder by shoulder.

"Here, you hungry?" He had peeled and quartered an orange; he held three sections out to her, half mushed. "I ate one," he said. Naturelle laughed and ate them from his palm. "Okay," he said. "You're in the home stretch. Just think: one hour and we'll be in a hot bath. I'll meet you in the park, right?"

"Yeah?"

"Shit, twenty-six miles. You're crazy." He patted her on the butt and she ran on, her mouth sweet with orange juice.

A beautiful day. Later they sat in the tub and Monty massaged her calves while she leaned back with her eyes closed. The hot water, Monty's hands, Aretha Franklin on the radio . . . Naturelle smiles, thinking back on it, then laughs out loud when she considers what an effort it was for Monty to be sweet. He couldn't keep it up for long. Holding her leg above the water, he ran his fingers over the Puerto Rican flag tattooed on her ankle.

"Not this again," she muttered, preempting him.

"You were born in America, you lived in America your whole life, you've been to Puerto Rico twice, for vacation. What is that? Should I get an Irish flag tattooed on my ass 'cause that's where my grandparents come from?"

"You don't have any *room* on your ass for a tattoo."

"Oh, is that right?" He poked her in the ribs. "Is that a fact?"

"Your skinny little white-boy ass," she told him, pinching his rear disdainfully.

"Between you and me, our kids will be just right."

Monty would joke about their future children; Naturelle never did. She could not imagine Monty as a father. She could easily imagine him impregnating women, but not being a father. The image of Montgomery walking through the park with a baby riding on his back was ludicrous, impossible.

Naturelle and Doyle finish their laps and run east from the reservoir. At Fifth Avenue she pulls the leash from her jacket pocket but Doyle slinks away. Naturelle knows what that slink means; she pulls a plastic bag from her jacket pocket and waits. She sees the tag SANE SMITH spray-painted across the base of a lamppost and remembers what Monty told her, that Sane Smith is dead, drowned in the East River.

When Doyle squats and fouls the clean curbside snow, he avoids looking at her; he always appears a little ashamed when he does his business. Naturelle wonders if Doyle was born a bashful dog or if bashfulness was beaten into him by his old masters. To this day he cringes when a stranger extends a hand meant for petting.

After the ritual is completed, they jog east to Lexington Avenue, where Naturelle ties Doyle to the post of a pay phone and walks into Papaya King. "Hey, Luis. Coconut champagne, please. Large."

Chewing on a straw, Naturelle sits on a stool and looks out through the glass door. Doyle waits in the snow, eyeing the passing pedestrians sadly. "Only a minute, Doyle," she whispers. Naturelle sips her sweet drink and watches the black dog shiver in the cold.

NINE

WHEN MONTY WAS twenty-two he almost helped murder the movie star Billy Marr. Monty had met Kostya a month before, at a dinner in one of Uncle Blue's restaurants in Brighton Beach. "From now on," Uncle Blue had said, wiping his beard with a red cloth napkin, "you two work together." He never explained why he thought such a partnership was a good idea or how they should divide their labors. Monty had disliked Kostya at first, irritated by the big man's constant clowning and bragging, the way he would get drunk and sing Bruce Springsteen songs on the street or kneel down in front of harried waitresses and recite Russian poetry from memory. But Kostya had called Monty "friend" the first night they met; he ignored Monty's surliness; he won Monty over with his certainty that they were meant to be comrades. Monty knew the Ukrainian was dangerous—at the Turkish baths one evening he had seen the ragged scar crossing Kostya's belly, and Kostya was the only man he knew who actually slept with an automatic beneath his pillow—but he needed a dangerous man on his side. Monty alone was too much of a target. There were hundreds of sugar bandits in New York, men who made their money robbing dealers. Dealers were sweet targets because they carried wads of cash and never called the police when they were rolled.

With Kostya, Monty had a bodyguard, someone whose very presence was intimidating.

They had gone to meet Billy Marr at his apartment in Chelsea. Monty slouched against the hallway wall, watching Kostya bang on the door and press the bell and mutter low oaths. After five minutes of this, a girl Monty guessed to be eighteen finally let them inside the place, a sprawling loft with bare concrete floors and ceilings twenty feet high. She wore a black silk robe, embroidered on the back with a Chinese dragon, and a green towel turbaned around her head. She led them into a sitting area and walked away without a word. All the furniture was white. A triptych of female nudes, painted in silver, hung above the fireplace. Three skinny young men slouched on a sofa, their forty-ounce bottles of beer cradled in their laps. They looked at Monty and Kostya for a moment and then returned their gaze to the television screen, to videotaped footage of air disasters: two propeller planes colliding above a runway; a fighter jet slamming into the prow of an aircraft carrier; a man whose parachute failed to open, falling, falling, falling. The camera watched him from the ground: the man started off a speck in the sky and grew larger and larger until, in the second before impact, his open mouth was clear and focused. He hit the desert floor so hard he bounced.

"Ouch," said Kostya. "You guys know where Billy Marr is?"

"Who are you?" said one of the skinnies, not looking up from the television.

"He called us," said Monty. "We're Uncle Blue's friends."

The girl in the black robe had reappeared, peeling a tangerine. The turban was gone. Her ash-blond hair was cut short. "Hey," she said, "the sugar man."

"Cool," said the talking skinny, sitting up. "Billy's not here, man. We'll hold on to it for him."

Monty ignored him and spoke to the girl. "Uncle said talk to Billy. You know when he's coming back?"

"He's out all night," she said, dropping the tangerine peels on the floor and halving the fruit. "How much is it? Gianni, you guys have any cash?"

The three young men made a half-hearted show of digging through their pockets.

"Twelve thousand dollars," said Monty. The three young men quit digging.

The girl shrugged, the movement causing the open V of the robe's lapels to flare farther apart. Monty caught a glimpse of white breast. He looked back to her bored blue eyes. He wanted the girl to offer him some tangerine but she never did.

"Why don't you just leave it here for him," she said. "He's good for it. It's Billy Marr."

Kostya laughed. "Not possible."

She spat a seed and began walking away. "You want to wait a few minutes, I can make some calls. He's one place or the other."

They ended up waiting an hour, taking the sofa when Gianni and his friends retreated to another room. Kostya put his arm around Monty's shoulders and spoke quietly into the younger man's ear. "Very stupid, what you did."

Monty could smell the mint of mouthwash on Kostya's breath and, below the mint, garlic. "What did I do?"

"We don't know these people from hole in the wall and you tell them, 'Twelve thousand dollars.' You tell them, 'We're friends with Uncle.' You never see them before and you tell them our business. Very stupid. Don't fuck me, okay, you hear? You know I have two strikes on me. Don't fuck me. I won't spend my life folding prison laundry."

They watched a hang glider slam into a cliff in Mexico, a helicopter plunge into a river, a military cargo jet's front tire burst on landing, sending the plane skidding on its nose into a hangar.

"Jesus Christ," said Kostya. "Who watches these things?"

At last the girl reemerged, wearing black nylon warm-ups and basketball shoes.

"He just called, he's at the Pierre. You guys have a car? I'll give you the room number."

"We have car," said Kostya, standing. "Let's meet Mister Movie Star."

When they got to Billy Marr's room on the fourth floor of the Pierre Hotel they found the door propped open with a room service cart. An uncracked lobster sat on a bed of seaweed, one dead antenna plunged into a bowl of congealed melted butter.

"Poor fuck," said Kostya. "Boiled for nothing."

They pushed the cart into the hallway and closed the door behind them. The room was dark. Billy Marr stood by the window, smoking a cigarette, watching headlights stream down Fifth Avenue. He wore a white T-shirt and black jeans. He was Monty's age, slender and fine-featured, famous for a smile that made women stupid with desire. But in the dark he was nondescript, a lean shadow. He turned and beckoned his guests closer.

"You guys are from here?"

"New York?" asked Monty.

Billy Marr laughed. "I figured you weren't from the Pierre Hotel."

"I am from Ukraine," said Kostya. "My friend, he is from New York."

"Where's the Dakota?" the actor asked, gesturing toward the window.

Monty pointed at the row of buildings on the far side of Central Park's dark sprawl. "One of those. I don't know which."

"That's where John Lennon lived with Yoko Ono. That's where he was shot. I want to take my girlfriend there tomorrow. John Lennon was God."

Half-assed God, thought Monty, getting himself shot on his own block.

"Listen, brothers," said Billy Marr, "I'm ready to sack out. Ten hours ago I was drunk in London."

"We're ready when you are," said Kostya, smiling, his false front teeth unnaturally white.

Billy Marr stared at them for a moment and then laughed. "Oh right, money. My brain's in England still." He slipped his wallet from his back pocket and pulled out a check.

Now it was Kostya's turn to laugh. "We don't take checks, Mr. Marr."

"You're kidding me." The actor frowned. "I always pay my guy in LA with checks."

Kostya shrugged. "Not for us, please."

"You think I can't cover this? I wipe my ass with twelve-thousand-dollar checks."

"We take American Express," said Monty.

"Really?"

"No, not really. We've been fucking around for three hours, looking for you. What is this?"

"Calm down," said Kostya, resting a heavy hand on Monty's shoulder.

"You know who I am?" asked the actor, squinting at Monty. "You know who you're talking to? I'm Billy Marr."

"I'm Montgomery Brogan."

"Yeah, great. Listen," the actor said to Kostya. "The money is not an issue. If there's a problem here, maybe there is, maybe it's a trust thing, but money is not the issue."

"The issue," said Kostya, "is money."

Billy Marr exhaled noisily, then jabbed his index finger into Monty's chest. "Let me show you something, brother. Come over here."

Kostya let go of Monty's shoulder and the three men walked over to a side door joining the suite's living room and bedroom. "Don't make any noise," said the actor, pushing the door open.

The television was on, blue-lighting a four-post bed: white sheets, chintz duvet, sleeping woman on her side. Billy Marr tiptoed over to her and studied her face. He slowly, slowly, pulled the sheet down the length of her body, exposing her in her naked sleep.

She was very beautiful, the bones of her face delicate in the lamplight. Her rib cage rose and fell with her breathing. Monty felt he should not be looking but he looked anyway: he studied her thighs, where they creased at her pelvis; her breasts, half covered by one arm; her mouth, lips slightly parted as if she were trying to speak in whatever dream now occupied her mind. Billy Marr smiled at Monty and Kostya. Monty turned around and left the bedroom.

Kostya followed a minute later, shaking his head. He huddled with Monty in the living room, whispering, "She looks like my cousin Zoya. I have shown you pictures, yes? The first girl I love, Zoya. She lose her arm in bad accident, very terrible, at factory. But still she is beautiful. One arm, but beautiful."

"That's Cassie Whitelaw."

"Who?"

"Cassie Whitelaw. She's on TV. You never seen her before? *St. James Infirmary*?"

" 'St. James Infirmary,' Louis Armstrong?"

"No, it's a TV show. She's a nurse; she's in love with one of the doctors."

"Hey," said Billy Marr, closing the bedroom door softly behind him. "You see what's waiting for me, brothers?"

"Your girlfriend?" asked Kostya.

"Twelve thousand dollars means nothing to me," said Billy Marr. "You comprehend what I'm saying?"

"No," said Kostya. "Not yet."

"I'm saying, don't go away with my sugar. We both have something the other guy wants. Am I wrong?"

Kostya frowned and stared at the closed suite door. "She is whore? She is beautiful, yes, but for twelve thousand dollars nobody is so beautiful."

"No," said the actor. "I'll give you the money tomorrow. This is by way of a down payment. She's a friend of mine. I tell her you're my old buddies; she'll help you out. She's not a whore, she's a fucking actress. She likes to party. All right? We have a deal?"

Monty spat on the floor. "You're a punk," he said, "pimping Cassie Whitelaw's ass."

"Are you insane? Do you know who the fuck you're talking to?"

"You're a punk and you've got no money and your movies suck."

Billy Marr started walking toward Monty, fists clenched. Monty waited and the actor stopped suddenly and laughed. "This is retarded. You're nothing, man. You're a penny-ante sugar man with some Russian goon for a bodyguard."

"Ukrainian," said Kostya.

"Tomorrow morning I fly to LA and a limousine picks me up at the airport. Tomorrow afternoon I'll be sitting poolside at my house sipping champagne in the sun, and you'll be standing on a corner selling junk to teenagers. That's your life. You're gone. The next time you see me, I'll be in a movie you're watching in jail. Some three-hundred-pound nigger will be cumming up your ass and you'll see my face on the television and I'll be smiling, motherfucker, I'll be laughing."

"Not if I shoot you tonight," said Kostya.

Billy Marr looked at the big man's face and blinked. "Hey," he said. "All right, hey. Let's call this a bad date, okay? This has all been a real bad blind date, and now we know better we won't do it again. Right?"

"My friend likes to shoot bad dates," said Monty. "That's the custom in the Ukraine."

Billy Marr said nothing for a moment. One of Kostya's hands was inside his coat pocket, and the actor watched the hand, shaking his head. "I'm going to bed. Okay? I'm going to bed, I'm going to sleep, and tomorrow none of us will remember this. Okay?" He pushed open the suite door and slipped through it, closing it and locking it behind him.

When Kostya and Monty left the room, Kostya grabbed the boiled lobster from the cart. He tried to shove it in his overcoat pocket but it didn't fit so he carried it while they rode down the elevator, while they strolled through the lobby, while they waited for the valet to bring their car.

"Hello, how are you?" asked Kostya, shaking hands with the lobster's claw. "Yes, yes, this movie star fuck you tonight, I know.

He fuck us too. But the woman, she was beautiful. If you had seen this woman, ah, maybe you die a little happy."

The valet pulled up with Monty's Corvette and Monty gave him a ten-dollar tip.

A year later Billy Marr drove over Cassie Whitelaw, crushing both her legs, after she tried to take the car keys from him following an eighteen-hour bender. He served six months in consequence, two of those months in a rehabilitation center in Northern California with hot tubs and a sand volleyball court.

TEN

THE WALK SIGN flashes and Slattery steps into the crosswalk. Jakob grabs his elbow. A jacked-up four-by-four careens around the corner at high speed, leaving a wake of bass-heavy radio music and an afterimage of happy faces, the driver and his laughing passengers.

"Saved your life," says Jakob, smiling. He is very pleased that *he* was the one who spied the oncoming car, that *he* was the one with the quick reactions, defying all expectations. But Slattery shows no gratitude; he stares furiously after the speeding truck.

"Did you see that? They were laughing at us! Little fucks almost kill us, and then they laugh at us!"

"Jerks," says Jakob. "Teenagers." He wonders if they were his students, a gang of juniors dissatisfied with their grades. Maybe Mary D'Annunzio paid them off.

"Those little punks." Slattery still stands by the curb, looking west through the falling snow toward where the truck disappeared. "Real tough guys behind two tons of steel."

Ten minutes later, seated at the window table of a Chinese restaurant, Slattery is still talking about it. "You get these kids who can't even write their own name, who were born in the *eighties*, for fuck's sake, and it's just like, Sure, here you go, here's a license for you to drive a big truck whenever you want, go for it, have fun, don't worry about that white stuff, that's just snow, go as fast as you want. You know? And if they just stayed out on the Island or in Jersey or wherever, fine, great, let them splatter themselves out there. But do they have to come into the city and risk *my* life?"

Jakob looks out the window. A woman battles her umbrella, trying to straighten the collapsed frame as snow collects in her red tangles of hair. He watches her struggle and falls in love with her. Jakob is forever falling in love with women he sees through windows, their unsmiling air of determination, grimly tramping to wherever they're going. Which is never to me, he thinks mournfully, and then rolls his eyes at his own self-pity. He pours tea for Slattery and himself.

The waiter comes over to take their order, scowl at their selections, and grab their menus without saying a word. Jakob imagines the waiter as the great poet of his generation, forced to flee China for supporting dissident causes, forced to make a living serving food without spice to men without talent.

Slattery gestures with his chin toward the window. "It's really coming down."

"They said we might get a foot," mumbles Jakob. He tries to divine the future in the swirling leaves at the bottom of his teacup. What will happen to Monty? Where is he now, out in the snow or warm inside, and what is he thinking, and is he afraid? He must be afraid, except Jakob cannot imagine Monty scared, cannot picture a look of fear on Monty's face. It's not courage, exactly—something is missing. Sometimes Jakob wonders if Monty believes in the reality of other people, the danger of other people.

Slattery watches his own spectral reflection in the window, a balding ghost in the falling snow. He looks at Jakob, at the crown of his fully haired head. What a waste, thinks Slattery.

"So I did the calculations the other day and you're in the sixty-second percentile."

Jakob looks up. "The what?"

"The sixty-second percentile. All the bachelors in New York, all the straight bachelors, we're competing for the women, right? It's like high school seniors competing for spots in the good colleges."

Jakob opens his mouth to speak, closes it, opens it again. "And I'm in the sixty-second percentile."

"Right."

"In other words, I'm better than sixty-two percent of the New York bachelors."

"You're rated higher than them, right."

"But worse than—what, thirty-eight percent?"

"Thirty-seven. There's no hundredth percentile."

The waiter arrives with a tray of aluminum-covered dishes. He arrays the dishes on the table and removes the covers: a sad pile of steaming greens on Jakob's side, heaps of glistening meats on Slattery's.

Jakob snaps apart his pair of wooden chopsticks. "How did you come up with sixty-two?"

"That's your rating. There's a whole way of figuring it."

"Oh, there's a whole way of figuring it. Well, that sounds fair. As long as there's a whole way of figuring it. And what are you? What's your rating?"

"Ninety-ninth percentile," says Slattery, picking up a dumpling with his fingers and dipping it in a puddle of soy sauce on his plate.

"Ha. So, okay, hold on a second. Who came up with these ratings?"

"I did."

"Oh, I see. You came up with the ratings. And you get a ninety-nine. That's very interesting. And what are they based on? What's the science behind this—"

"Don't get all annoyed," says Slattery, through a mouthful of ground pork and scallions. "It's a system. It's not saying you're a bad person."

"Just a bad bachelor."

"No. A better-than-average bachelor." Slattery blows steam into his cupped hands. "Hot. You ordered all these vegetables and you're not eating any."

Jakob stabs a mustard green with one chopstick. "So what are the criteria?"

"You want some dumpling? . . . Okay, first off, money. You make none. That right there keeps you out of the top ten percent."

"Ten percent of what? Ten percent of the gold diggers."

"Ten percent, period. Two, you're short. No offense, but a lot of women won't go out with anybody shorter than them. Why are you getting so mad? It's a fact. What are you, five-six?"

"I'm five-eight."

"You are not five-eight."

Jakob uses his chopstick as a catapult to hurl a mustard green at Slattery's face; Slattery grabs the leaf in midair and stuffs it in his mouth.

"Fuck you," says Jakob, but it doesn't sound right. There is a hesitancy in Jakob's cursing, a hitch before his fucks and shits; the words come across as self-consciously selected. The speech of Monty and Slattery is rife with profanity, but for them it sounds entirely natural.

Slattery shrugs. "It's just facts, man. Don't let it get you down."

But Jakob is down. In high school he convinced himself that he was a late bloomer, the Pimpled Virgin, a type played in movies by funny-looking kids with braces who trip through the first reel, bullied and insulted, but lose their V to beauties before the credits roll. Jakob feels he has the right to that ending; he has been waiting patiently for ten years. Not that he's a virgin—Jakob has slept with three separate women, all of them kind and vaguely attractive—but *three*? Twenty-six years old and only three women? He knows he shouldn't think of it statistically; he is not chasing Hank Aaron's home-run record. But it's hard when your best friends are getting laid sophomore year of high school and you're watching the nude talk show on channel J; it's hard teaching *The Great Gatsby* and talking about Daisy and realizing that your teenage students get more action than you do; it's hard still playing the Pimpled Virgin at age twenty-six, minus the pimples, minus the virginity.

For the past three weeks, the nightly jerk-off has starred Mary

D'Annunzio, which makes Jakob feel sick at heart. I'm not a pervert, he tells himself, but he has a hard time believing it. She's too young, he knows she's too young, he knows he will not lay hands on her, but Christ, she's a squatter in his skull. If I wait three years? he thinks. I could wait that long. Travel up to whatever college she's at, find her name in the student directory. And then . . . what? Would I just call her? What would I say?

Hi, Mary? Mary D'Annunzio? This is—do you recognize my voice? No? It's Mr. Elinsky! From Campbell-Sawyer.

Oh, Jesus, thinks Jakob, that's pathetic. I'd have to find out where she was living and then, somehow or other, arrange to bump into her.

Mary? Mary D'Annunzio? My God, what are you doing here? You go here, that's right, I completely. . . . Oh, I'm just visiting some friends. What a nice surprise, running into you. . . . Excuse me? . . . Of course, you can tell me anything you'd like. . . . No, tell me, tell me. I'm good at keeping secrets. . . . You had a huge crush on me? Really? . . . No, no, don't be embarrassed, it's . . . well, I don't know if lots of girls did. Maybe a couple.

"What are you grinning about?" asks Slattery.

"What puts you in the ninety-ninth percentile? That's what I'm wondering."

"Okay, I'm—"

"Aside from your salary."

Slattery hesitates. "Well . . ."

"Doesn't losing your hair drop you down a few places?"

"Nope, not at all. It would only bother women if it bothered me."

"It does bother you," says Jakob.

"No, it doesn't."

"Of course it does. If it didn't bother you, you wouldn't smear that goop all over your scalp twice a day."

Jakob knows it's dangerous to push the point when Slattery starts looking at you like that, looking at you like you're a small bug crawling across the television screen, but Jakob also knows he can get away with it. Slattery will never smack him. Still, Jakob re-members the time Slattery lost a wrestling match in overtime, sen-ior year, his first match as captain of the team. Afterward they sat next to each other in the locker room, Jakob trying to console his friend. Slattery rocked back and forth, eyes closed, a white towel draped over his head, sweat running off his bare back. He groaned, a long, low groan, then leaned forward and struck the facing locker with his left hand. He left the room in silence, headed for the showers, leaving Jakob alone on the wooden bench staring at a caved-in locker, the upper hinges snapped clean off.

Using his fingers, Slattery picks an uncooked grain from his fried rice, inspects it, and flicks it away. "The hair is a nonissue."

"Are table manners an issue? The shiny thing to the left of your plate, that's a fork. When people eat rice they use chopsticks or a fork—a spoon, whatever—but grown people do not eat fried rice with their fingers. You have no idea how to behave. You spend the whole week figuring out how to defraud foreign governments, or whatever you do, and when you get out of there, when you're in this strange world outside the office called *reality*, you have no idea how to behave. So what's Monty? How does he rate on your lit-tle scale?"

"Monty? Monty's going to prison. He's a flat zero." Slattery lifts himself half out of his chair and stretches his left leg until he hears a small *pop!*

"Are you all right?" asks Jakob. "The war wounds?"

But Slattery's face is dark, his nostrils flared. "Those little punks nearly killed me."

"Who?"

"Those punks in the four-by-four. They tried to run me over."

"You're going to obsess on this all night, aren't you?"

"I would love to get my hands on them. Oh, Jesus. We'll see how tough they are. Let me have each of them in a locked room for five minutes. Just give me five minutes. Then we'll see."

"Come on, eat your spareribs. They're getting cold." I'm sur-rounded by maniacs, thinks Jakob. The waiter lives here in furious exile; my best friend is a berserker; the man passing by the window is heading home to murder his wife. It's a city of maniacs. What am I doing here?

But Jakob knows he will never leave New York. He lived in Seattle for one year after college, and it didn't take. He felt like such a stereotype of his generation—working at a coffee shop, for God's sake, even trying to grow a goatee. After a while he realized that he didn't really like the music he told everyone he liked; that proximity to thousands of miles of mountain biking trails did not, in fact, give him hard-ons of anticipation; that the company of his tattooed and pierced fellow espresso grinders made him feel like an extra in a music video already outdated. He went home for the Seder and realized he longed for the city and that *city* would always mean one place for him. Everywhere he went people begged for his return. Come back, said the beauty in leather pants working the register of a Madison Avenue boutique; come back, sang the ornery token clerks in the Union Square subway station; come back, called the hot-dog vendors outside the Metropolitan Museum; come back, Jakob, come back, the whole city shouted, come back, we'll spell your name with window lights on the Empire State Building.

Slattery broods over his plate of bones, the corners of his lips twitching. "So how's work going?" Jakob asks. He figures he ought to distract his friend from the angry fantasies. It seems as if Slattery is always grumpiest during cold weather: every winter of high school he starved himself to make weight, and every winter of college. He hasn't gotten over it yet.

Slattery says nothing for a few seconds. Then: "Beautiful. Everyone loves me."

"You have mustard on your chin," says Jakob.

Slattery wipes it off with the back of his hand. "We got to get out of here. I told Monty we'd meet him at ten." He catches the waiter's eye and pantomimes signing a check.

"That's eleven-thirty, M.B.T."

"Tell you what, Montgomery Brogan Time is about over. He's going on Government Time in a few hours."

Jakob shakes his head and watches the Sixth Avenue traffic roll through the snow. "It just doesn't seem fair to me."

"What doesn't?"

"Some guy stabs his wife in the face," says Jakob, "and he gets out in three years. Monty's never been in trouble before, he doesn't shoot anyone, he doesn't hit anyone over the head with a baseball bat, and he'll be in there for seven years? It's not right."

Slattery takes the check from the waiter, quickly tallies the figures, and hands over his credit card.

"How much do I owe?" asks Jakob.

"I got it."

"Why? No, come on, I can pay for my—"

"I got it, Jake. Don't worry about it."

Jakob slumps back in his chair. "Anyway, it doesn't seem fair to me."

"You've made that point. You've been saying the same thing for the last two weeks. And you're full of shit."

"I'm full of shit? Wait, you think this is justice? You think Monty deserves—"

"Hey, I sat next to you at Aaron Haddad's funeral. You remember his mother? They practically had to carry her in."

"I remember."

"The pew we were sitting in was shaking. All through the service, this pew was shaking. And I was thinking, There's no subway underneath us, we're on Madison Avenue. So why is the pew shaking? And then I looked over, and it was these three girls, three cute girls, crying their eyes out. They were sobbing so hard the whole pew was shaking. Well, the shit that killed Aaron is the same shit Monty sells. So don't sit there and tell me how unfair it is poor Monty's going away."

The waiter returns to their table with the credit card receipt. Slattery signs his name and pockets his copy.

"When I found out about Aaron," says Jakob, "I didn't think, Boy, I hope they find the guy who sold him that stuff. I thought, That stupid jerk, he threw it all away. Nobody made Aaron do anything. He made a choice, and he blew it. You know what? I'm sorry, I know this sounds mean, but fuck him. Mike Feaney got bone cancer, it took him four years to die, and he was fighting the whole time. And Aaron just throws it away. Fuck him."

"Fine, and fuck his mother too. The kid made a mistake. Guess what, Jake, that's what kids do. That doesn't make him evil."

"I didn't say it made him evil," says Jakob.

"It doesn't make him deserve to die. How many times in college did I get flat drunk and drive somewhere for a pizza? Every weekend? And if I had gotten squashed on the freeway, would you be saying, Fuck him, he deserved it?"

"If you got killed drunk driving, yeah, I'd think you were a stupid jerk. But I'd still miss you. And I wouldn't go blaming the bartender for selling you the beer."

Slattery closes his eyes and pinches the bridge of his nose. "Don't bullshit me. Monty made money off people's addiction. He was driving a Corvette paid for by addiction. You can hand me whatever line of crap you want, but that's the truth. And he got caught, and he's going away, and you know what? He's my best friend in the world—you and him are my best friends in the world—and I love him like a brother, and he fucking deserves it."

But Jakob knows there can only be one best friend, only one best man at the wedding. He throws up his hands. "Fine. Are you going to tell him that? Are you going to say, *Hey, Monty, sorry about tomorrow, brother, but you deserve it?*"

"No," says Slattery, standing. "I'm telling you and it stays between us. Let's go get him."

ELEVEN

"WATCH ME," SAYS Kostya. He ducks his head and throws two left jabs, his ringed fist flashing through the air. "You see? Very straight line. You don't want to come around in circle. This is what you see in movies, yes? Sylvester Stallone throwing *bi-i-i-g* punch like this—" He demonstrates the improper roundhouse. "You want speed, yes? Speed. What is fastest way from point A to point B?"

"Straight line," says Volandes.

"Straight line. Yes. Point A is my fist now; point B is other man's chin. You see? Wait, I don't want to sweat on shirt." Kostya begins unbuttoning his orange silk shirt. "This shirt I got in Miami."

"Come on, you got to get naked in my office?" Volandes sits at his desk in his cramped, windowless office, hands behind his head. The walls are covered with framed photographs of Volandes with minor New York celebrities: the weatherman for a local television station, the Bronx borough president, a New York Yankees catcher, a radio deejay, models, actors, and singers. In all these pictures Volandes, a small man with a mane of curly black hair, wears the same gap-toothed grin, the nightclub manager's grin. The celebrities smile wearily for the camera.

"You know nothing about fine clothes, my friend. Never sweat in silk." Kostya folds the shirt carefully and lays it on Volandes's bare desk.

"I don't wear silk. Too hard to clean. You're getting fat, Novotny." Volandes cannot keep his eyes off the leather holster strapped to the small of Kostya's back, the black steel butt of an automatic peeking out.

"Silk is like skin of virgin's thigh," says Kostya, stretching his thick arms above his head. "Women see man in silk, they know he has class. They know he has money. Now watch."

Volandes laughs. "They know he has class because he's wearing the skin of a virgin's thigh?"

"Watch. American boxers, they learn to fight in ghetto. They are street fighters. Some are very good street fighters, but there is no science, no art. This is American boxer." Kostya throws a left-right-left combination, his head held high. "Good punches, yes, but look." He repeats the combination, his hairy belly slowly swaying. "No defense. You see? Face is—"

"Unprotected."

"Yes, face is unprotected. And body! American boxers, they never attack body. Everybody wants knockout. They want one big punch. No discipline, these fighters. Where I am from, Ukraine, we train from very small and we learn technique. American fighters, very good athletes. But technique, no."

"So how come there's no champions from the Ukraine?" asks Volandes.

"Amateur champions we have. But our boxers fight in other countries only last five, six years. Soon we have champion."

"Not you, though, buddy. Not with that gut."

Kostya shrugs. "Women like men with meat. You see this?" He fingers a long ridged scar running down from his navel under the waistband of his wool trousers. "When I was twelve I catch soldier raping my mother. I scream, I punch him, try to kick his balls. He takes knife and opens me up. My mother, she is trying to push me back in. My—how do you say, the coils—" Kostya twirls his finger to indicate coils.

"Intestines?"

"My intestines come falling out. So she is pushing them back in. Very bad. But see—" Kostya beats his chest with his fist. "I survive. Big man, now. Later, I find out he was not raping my mother. So, okay, he wasn't such a bad man. He drove me to hospital."

"After he cut you up?"

"Yes, but he felt very bad. I scared him. He comes back from Afghanistan. Things very bad there for Soviet soldiers. So yes, he cuts me up, but then he drives me to hospital and we become friends."

Volandes whistles. "I thought the Bronx was fucked."

"This man, this soldier, now he is my father-in-law."

"Your father-in-law?"

"No, no, how do you say, he marries my mother—"

"Stepfather?"

"Stepfather! Yes. He is my stepfather. Still in Ukraine, with my mother. Good man. I send them money; they live well. No money in Ukraine."

"Speaking of money," says Volandes, "tell me about tonight."

"Women love scars," says Kostya, rubbing the puckered skin.

"You know all about women, don't you? You know so much about women, how come you always go home with some cow at five in the morning?"

"Women love scars," repeats Kostya. "They know a man has been somewhere, he has scars."

"So what you're telling me—I want to see if I got this right. What you're telling me is women love fat scarred guys in silk? Acne scars, do they count?" Volandes runs his hands over his pockmarked jaw. "The fat I got. Okay, tell me the plan for tonight."

"We need VIP room. Give me two staff in there. Who's on door, Khari?"

"It's a Thursday night. You want me to close off the VIP room for the whole night?"

"Uncle Blue wants VIP room."

Volandes sighs. "All right. That's what he wants; it's his place.

We're getting a crowd tonight. This deejay I got playing, some kid from Queens, he's like Jesus Christ these days. Everywhere he goes there's a crowd following him. Every high school kid in the five boroughs is going to be at the door tonight."

Kostya picks up his orange shirt and slides his arm through the sleeve. "Underage? Very dangerous. You want police in here?"

"No," says Volandes. "I said at the door. I didn't say they were getting in."

"Khari's working the VIP room tonight?"

"No, Khari's working the front. I need him out there, with the mess we're going to have. If you had told me about this earlier, I would have said do it another night. Everything's crazy when this deejay plays."

"Another night?" asks Kostya, buttoning his shirt and tucking it inside his pants. "Montgomery goes to prison tomorrow. You want we should give him party tomorrow night?"

"How about last night? Last night was empty."

Kostya frowns. "My friend goes to prison tomorrow for seven years. You talk about crowded? About your deejay?"

"All right," says Volandes, raising his hands. "I'm sorry. I like Monty; he's a good kid. Okay, two VIP staff. I'll put Oscar on VIP door. Girls?"

"Two girls. Maybe three. He likes—he likes everything, but mostly short, dark. Puerto Ricans. He likes Puerto Ricans."

"That's easy." Volandes picks up the phone and pushes a button. "Get Roz and Maggie in here. . . . Huh? Where is she? . . . Oh, Christ. Well track her down, would you? Tell Roz to come in here." He replaces the phone in its cradle.

"Champagne," says Kostya. "He loves champagne."

"What do you think, six bottles?"

"Two cases. Cristal."

Volandes smiles. "He's got expensive tastes, that Monty. You want Cristal, I need to hear it from Uncle. That stuff is too—"

Kostya rests his heavy hands on Volandes's desk and studies the little man's face. "My friend goes to Otisville tomorrow for seven years. You sit here—"

"All right," says Volandes.

"Two cases."

"All right. What else?" Volandes taps the side of his nose.

"No," says Kostya. "None of that."

A slender woman with copper skin and bleached-blond hair enters the room.

"Oh, Christ, Roz," says Volandes. "What did you do to your head?"

"I dye my hair yesterday."

"You dye your hair yesterday. That's great. Who told you to do that? All right, forget it. You're in luck tonight—you're going to meet a friend of ours. Our friend, he looks like a movie star. What are you, Puerto Rican?"

"Yemeni," she says.

"Yemeni?" Volandes raises his eyebrows. "All right whatever, tell him you're Puerto Rican. Our friend loves Latinas."

"I'm not Puerto Rican."

"I know you're not Puerto Rican. Let's make it easy for you. Just keep your mouth shut when you're with him, okay? No, hey, shut up. Start practicing now. No talkie, all right?"

"Yemen," says Kostya. "Yemen borders Saudi Arabia and Oman. Yes?"

Roz smiles. "You are not American."

"I am from Ukraine."

"Americans," says Roz, "they know where nothing is."

"Yeah," says Volandes. "Yemen and Ukraine are so wonderful, how come you both came here?"

"Education in America," says Kostya, "is very bad. You do not know your own history. Do you know even when was your civil war?"

"It wasn't my civil war," says Volandes. "My parents came here in 1959."

"This shirt," says Roz, rubbing the fabric of Kostya's shirt between her thumb and forefinger, "very nice."

"You like? Silk."

"Very nice."

"This shirt I buy in Hong Kong. Hong Kong, they make best shirts anywhere."

"They make pretty good shirts in Miami too," says Volandes.

"Your friend," says Roz. "Is he a famous actor?"

Kostya nods. "Very famous. Many movies. You like movies?"

"I like good movies."

"I think," says Kostya, "maybe you and me have fun tonight."

"You and me and friend?" Roz looks at Volandes and shakes her head. "No, too much."

"No," says Kostya, "just you and me." He draws a stuffed money clip from his rear pocket and drops it on Volandes's desk. "We have fun tonight. Let me show you this," he says, unbuttoning his shirt.

"What are you doing?" asks Volandes. "You want to drink all the champagne now, too?"

"She's not Puerto Rican. Montgomery hates Yemenis."

Volandes shakes his head and picks up the phone again. "Hey, you found her yet? . . . Oh, Christ. Every week I got to deal with this. Would you find me a couple Puerto Rican girls, please? . . . What? What? We're in fucking New York City, how hard can it be? Two Puerto Rican girls. And, hey, call Eddie, make sure we have six bottles of Cristal reserved for the VIP room." Volandes looks up and sees that Kostya is talking with Roz, pinching her waist. "Non-vintage."

Kostya removes his shirt again, sucking his belly flat. "I was boxer," he tells Roz. "Here, touch my nose."

Roz rubs Kostya's flattened nose. "Yes," she says. "The greatest boxer of all is Yemeni. Prince Naseem."

"You see this?" he asks her, pointing to his long scar.

"Yes, what do you say this? Cut?"

"Scar," says Kostya. He leans down and whispers into her ear. "Scar."

Roz smiles. She runs her fingertips along the length of the scar, from the navel to where it disappears below his belt-line. Kostya smiles at Volandes. "Big scar."

"Big man," says Roz, patting Kostya's thick arm. "Very big man."

"Yes," says Kostya, making a muscle. "Big man."

TWELVE

MONTGOMERY LOVES HIS city best when the snow is falling, when the sidewalks are tracked with overlapping footprints and the tops of tall buildings are swallowed by clouds. The cars on Houston spin their wheels when the light changes, swerving and sliding and sounding their horns. Monty forgot to wear proper boots for the weather; he can feel the wet seeping through the fine leather of his shoes. But his camel's-hair overcoat keeps his body dry, and his knit watch cap keeps his head warm. Monty stares into the faces of every man and woman he passes. He wonders where they are going, what they have planned for the night. An Indian couple strolls by, arm in arm, the man holding a black umbrella over their heads with his free hand. Monty hears only the accent, English, and one word, *irredeemable*. The woman said it, emphasis on *deem*, a tone of accusation but not against her companion, against someone or something else, and Monty wants to know what stands accused, movie or boss or girlfriend.

Wherever you sleep tonight, woman, wherever you lay your head, that is where I want to be. Inside the walls is a tangle of faulty wiring, set to spark and flare when the time is right, and you will sleep through the stink of melted copper and burning plaster, you will sleep through the small grabbing hands of the first flames, until the curtains ignite and smoke begins rolling across the ceiling and you finally open your eyes. I will come for you then, when the wallpaper is bubbling on the walls. I will walk through the burning doorway, one step ahead of the collapsing ceiling. I will lift you from your bed and carry you to the window, hoist you over my shoulder, climb down the fire escape, and leave you with the medics. Because it's true: I would have been a wonderful fireman.

Monty stops before the window of a bakery. He has passed this shop before, has seen Naturelle look sadly at the pastries and stomp away. He stares at the confections stacked on silver trays, a lush display of sweets beckoning to passersby: the puff pastries and peekaboo tarts, the chocolate éclairs and pecan pies, the meringue cookies and madeleines, the strawberry tartlets and honey-spice cakes. Monty has never been less hungry, but he admires the artfulness, the order. He wonders who created this arrangement, who sat inside the window and positioned each dessert in its proper place, with an eye for the colors and forms. And he wonders where she is now, for Monty is sure it's a woman. He imagines her standing in a high apartment, looking down at the city, still dressed in her baker's white uniform, her fingertips dark with dried chocolate. *Bake me a cake, lady.*

He turns from the window and heads east. A young athlete in his varsity jacket sprints past, thick-necked and crew-cut, a bouquet of red roses in plastic wrap held close to his chest. I could take her from you, thinks Monty. I could follow you right now to wherever you're meeting, to the red Naugahyde booth where she sits waiting, slide next to her, and steal her away. Monty knows she would come; he knows the words. Or maybe not, a girl dating Mr. Crew-cut-and-red-roses is not exactly Montgomery-style; still, there's always a chance. Their eyes would meet for one lingering moment and he would know the odds.

Monty cannot remember a time when women did not fuss over him. He has always been pretty. Growing up in Bensonhurst, Monty had to prove his toughness wherever he was unknown. His eyes were too green, his lashes too long, his nose too delicate. Boys did not trust him, not at first. When he was younger, Monty went out of his way to obscure his looks. He would wear baseball caps to hide his thick, dark hair. He never smiled because his teeth were perfect, absolutely straight without need for braces. But the disguises never worked; he still stood out, and kids went after him. So Monty fought, and he fought well. There is little art to an adolescent fistfight. Monty swung first, he swung hard, and he never let up. He shrugged off whatever blows he took in return. A black eye was a mark of courage; it let the other boys know he would not be pushed around.

Later, Monty realized his face could be useful. Girls he passed on the street would nudge each other and giggle. Older women, teachers and friends' mothers, would fawn over him, listening to his every word, especially when they heard that his own mother was gone. Many of his classmates in high school resented his status as resident lady-killer, but they were quiet in their resentment. In Bensonhurst, Monty was considered a stand-up kid, willing to fight for respect but by no means an intimidator. At Campbell-Sawyer, where months went by without a punch being thrown, Monty became legendary for his ferocity.

In his sophomore year he was named starting point guard for the varsity basketball team. During one important league game an opposing forward hacked Monty constantly. Every time Monty drove to the basket, the forward clobbered him, using his elbows and his hips. The referees called a few fouls but missed several others, and Monty grew increasingly angry, until one play when he jumped for a rebound and felt his legs swept out from under him. He hit the floor hard, back first. He stood up swinging. The forward had been waiting for this all night and was ready. He outweighed Monty by forty pounds and stood several inches taller. By the time the coaches and referees pulled the combatants apart, it was clear that Monty was losing the fight. Both players were thrown out of the game, but first the coaches insisted that they shake hands. The forward offered his and Monty punched him hard in the mouth, knocking the larger boy to the floor.

He was kicked off the team and, without basketball, began to lose interest in school life. Classwork, which had come easily for him in his old schools, required intense study now, and Monty was only capable of bursts of intensity. In the spring of his sophomore year, eating pizza with seniors during lunch break, he listened to them discuss their plans to buy a bag of marijuana. One of the boys said they would need eighty dollars, and Monty, barely paying attention, said, "You're getting ripped off."

"Yeah? How much do you pay?"

Monty shrugged, as if he were used to haggling for the merchandise, though at that point he had never bought or sold drugs in his life, or even considered such a possibility. "I could get it to you for half that," he said. And so the seniors gave him forty dollars, and Monty, knowing his reputation as a street-smart kid was on the line, talked to some friends in Bensonhurst and delivered on time. He ended up spending an extra twenty dollars of his own money, but soon all of the seniors were coming to him, and Monty quickly began turning a profit.

Near the end of his junior year, the coaches at Campbell-Sawyer learned about Monty's business from a few of the younger athletes. The administration was informed and one afternoon, after lunch, Monty's locker was opened and a brown paper bag discovered, filled with prescription painkillers and ecstasy tablets. The next day he was officially "separated" from the school, barred permanently from the grounds. A letter was sent to all parents, discreetly urging them to prevent their children from associating with Montgomery Brogan. Because the computer files had not yet been updated, one copy of the letter was accidentally sent to Mr. Brogan, who drove into Manhattan and threatened the headmaster with a lawsuit or a beating or both, never believing his son might actually be a criminal.

Campbell-Sawyer had not seen so much excitement in years, not since the head of the History Department was caught fellating the editor of the yearbook in a bathroom stall, but if Monty was distraught he did not show it. He never tried to find out who had betrayed him—what would be the point? He cleared out his locker, said his goodbyes, and left.

By the time his friends were proceeding past the podium in their mortarboards and black gowns, Monty had rented his own Yorkville apartment, leased a Corvette, and saved enough money to throw the most lavish graduation party of the year, summoning all his ex-classmates to a grand club forty stories above the street. Waiters circulated bearing trays of champagne flutes. Belly dancers brushed by the tuxedoed boys. Monty sauntered from room to room, escorted by the most beautiful sixteen-year-old girl from all of Bensonhurst, a blue-eyed brunette; her father and brothers were police officers who believed that Monty was a freshman at Columbia.

Among the teenagers gathered there that night, preparing for a summer of beach parties and bong sessions before heading off to college, Montgomery was already a legend, an outlaw hipster. Everyone knew the stories: the time he ran across the subway tracks to kiss a girl on the opposite platform; the time he slugged an opponent on the basketball court (in the later versions, Monty broke the other boy's jaw with a single punch); the time he seduced the French teacher, Mlle. Cendrars, and left her sprawled naked and purring in the audiovisual room (a myth invented by Jakob Elinsky, who spent much of his senior year in the library bathroom masturbating to Mlle. Cendrars but could not, even in his fantasies, conceive of *himself* and the Frenchwoman getting it on).

The party became legend. Whenever Monty runs into an alumnus from Campbell-Sawyer, the man will always mention that night, and the belly dancers . . . "and who was that girl you were with, the brunette? Jesus, whatever happened to her?" What happened to her was her brothers checked Columbia's student directory, found no listing for Montgomery Brogan, surmised Monty's true profession, and told their sister she would no longer be seeing the Black Irish kid. She locked herself in her room and went on a hunger strike for three days, but Monty let it go, deciding it was best to dissociate himself from a family of angry cops.

Donatella Bruno. Where is she now? Monty wonders. He stops in his tracks and brushes snow from his collar. He pats the small of his back, feeling for the hard ridge of metal below the camel's-hair, the holstered pistol strapped to his belt. Monty loves his .40; he thrills to its weight, the purity of its lines, its simplicity of purpose. Walking with a gun is walking with power. He taught himself to shoot at a Brooklyn firing range, blasting at targets alongside his father, who keeps an ancient Browning 9-millimeter under his bar. Monty's black leather holster was hand-tooled by a gnomish Calabrian in Bensonhurst: a large *B* for Brogan, patterned after the old Brooklyn Dodgers insignia.

Monty stares through another plate-glass window, through letters spelled in gold script, into a restaurant of white-clothed tables in buttery light, the people inside warm and comfortable and well fed, bottles of red wine by their breadbaskets. The hostess is on the telephone, laughing, twirling a pen around her fingertips.

Where am I going? Monty asks himself. To meet my friends at a bar? What will we do, sit around drinking, telling old stories? What the hell are we going to do? And what could be more pathetic than the awkward silences, the pledges of solidarity, the earnest and pitiful companionship?

He opens the restaurant door and presents himself to the hostess, his watch cap in his hands. She murmurs *bon soir* into the telephone receiver and hangs up.

"Good evening," she says.

She isn't beautiful, thinks Monty, but she has presence: tall, elegant, gray-eyed, and European. The words *bon soir* linger like an exotic fragrance.

"Good evening," says Monty, staring at her. He has forgotten the words. This is his game and he has forgotten how to play. He stares at her and she smiles, casts her eyes down, and pencils a name onto the reservations chart.

This is it, Monty tells himself. He reviews the old tactics and settles on a classic.

"I've got a theory," he tells the woman. *First you hook them. Not aggressive, not pushy. Get them curious.* "My theory—tell me if I'm wrong—I've got this theory that it doesn't really matter what a guy says to a woman: the first line, I mean. It doesn't matter, he could recite the Lord's Prayer, whatever, she's already made up her mind."

The hostess cocks one eyebrow. "The Lord's Prayer?"

"She's already decided. By the time he's opened his mouth, she's already decided, yes or no, thumbs up or down. Tell me if I'm wrong."

She shakes her head slowly. "She's already decided if he has a chance. But she's waiting to be convinced."

"Right, fair enough. Within reason. So if I said I wanted to see you again, if I said I wanted to take you out one night, what would you think?"

"What would I think? Or what would I say?"

"What would you say?"

"I'd say I have a boyfriend."

"Oh."

"Are you here for dinner?" she asks, smiling.

Monty kneads the cap in his hands, the clumps of snow melting on the wool. "I already ate." Now he feels stupid, a failed Romeo dripping on the carpet. "Could I use your bathroom for a minute?"

The hostess wasn't expecting that question. "You came in here to use the bathroom?"

"No. I came in here to ask you out. But now I have to pee."

"In the back," she says, pointing, and she watches him weave through the tables, touching a waiter's shoulder when he needs to pass by.

Monty locks the door of the small bathroom and sits on the closed toilet seat. Someone has written *Fuck you* in silver marker above the roll of toilet paper. Sure, he thinks. And fuck you too. Fuck everyone. The French hostess, the diners drinking wine, the waiters taking orders. Fuck this city and everyone in it. The panhandlers, grinning on the street corners, begging for change. The turbaned Sikhs and unwashed Pakistanis racing their yellow cabs

down the avenues. The Chelsea faggots with their waxed chests
and pumped-up biceps. Fuck them all. The Korean grocers with
their pyramids of overpriced fruit, their plastic-wrapped tulips and
roses. The white-robed Nigerians selling counterfeit Gucci on
Fifth Avenue. The Russians in Brighton Beach, drinking their tea
from glasses, sugar cubes clenched between their teeth. Fuck them.
The black-hatted Hasidim in their dirty gabardine suits, selling di-
amonds on 47th Street, counting their money while they wait for
Meshiach. The sidewalk gimps, bodies crooked and spastic. The
Wall Street brokers, smug and cologned, reading their folded papers
in subway cars. Fuck them all. The skateboard punks in Washington Square Park, wallet chains rattling as they leap the curb. The
Puerto Ricans, flags flying and radios howling from the open windows of their cars. The Bensonhurst Italians pomading their hair,
with their nylon warm-up suits and St. Anthony medallions. The
Upper East Side wives, with their pinched mouths and lifted faces,
with their scarves from Hermès and their artichokes from Bal-
ducci's. Fuck the uptown brothers, they never pass the ball, they
don't play defense, they take four steps on every drive to the hoop.
Fuck the prep school junkies, smoking tar in Daddy's kitchen
while the old man jets to Tokyo. Fuck the police, the bullyboys in
blue with their thick-necked swagger, zooming through red lights
on their way to Krispy Kreme. Fuck the Knicks—Patrick Ewing
and his blown finger roll against Indiana, Charles Smith and his
failed layups against Chicago, John Starks and his thousand missed
shots against Houston—fuck them, they'll never beat Jordan, they
will never beat Jordan. Fuck Jakob Elinsky, that whining runt.
Fuck Frank Slattery, always staring at my girlfriend's ass. Fuck Naturelle Rosario, set free tomorrow when I'm gone. Fuck Kostya
Novotny; I trusted him and he dimed me out. Fuck my father,
alone in his darkroom, hanging wet prints from a line. Fuck my
mother, rotting below the snow. Fuck Jesus Christ, he got off easy,
an afternoon on the cross, a weekend in hell, and then the hallelu-
jahs of all the legioned angels. Fuck this city and everyone in it—
from the row houses of Astoria to the duplexes of Park Avenue,

from the projects in Brownsville to the lofts in Soho, from Belle-vue Hospital to the tenements in Alphabet City to the brown-stones in Park Slope—let the Arabs bomb it all to rubble; let the waters rise and submerge the whole rat-crazed place; let an earth-quake tumble the tall buildings; let the fires reign uncontested; let it burn, let it burn, let it burn. And fuck you, Montgomery Bro-gan, you blew it.

Someone is banging on the bathroom door and Monty stands, walks over to the sink, and washes his hands. He stares at his face in the mirror. For all the good it did you, he thinks. Green eyes, high cheekbones, straight nose, perfect white teeth. Pretty white boy. Eyes, bones, nose, teeth. More banging on the door. And Monty knows what he has to do. "Fuck it," he whispers, and waves goodbye to the face in the mirror.

THIRTEEN

UNCLE BLUE CARVES open the middle of his steak with his wood-handled knife and examines the meat. The sirloin is over-cooked, the center pink instead of red, and Uncle Blue beckons for his waiter with one finger. The waiter rushes over.

"This is not rare. Please bring me another."

"Right away, I'm sorry about that. I wrote down rare."

"Fine. And another glass of wine."

Uncle Blue's companion is a deeply tanned man wearing a handsome blue suit, his white cuffs projecting an exact inch beyond his jacket's sleeves, his fingernails buffed and neatly trimmed. A plate of grilled octopus sits before him.

"Please," says Uncle Blue, "eat."

"You'd think when you own a place, they'd cook your steak right." The tanned man squeezes lemon over his octopus. "This looks good, though."

"I hope so, Mr. Gedny. I taught the chef how to make it."

"Mm. Very nice. They give you a lot, too. Lots of octopuses. Octopi?"

Uncle Blue smiles. "Either way. The servings are not usually so large; we wouldn't make a profit."

"But I'm eating with the boss." Gedny wipes his mouth clean

with his napkin and looks out the window. "Look at that stuff come down. My car's going to get buried."

They sit in the private balcony of the restaurant. Whitewashed walls, clay tile floors, bright posters of the Parthenon at sunset and Santorini at dawn. The tables in the main room below—glass tops supported by miniature Doric columns—are empty and un-clothed; diners stayed home tonight, not willing to drive or walk through a blizzard.

"You met with Brogan this morning?" asks Uncle Blue.

"I did, yeah."

"How did he seem?"

Gedny reaches for his wine. "He's not loving life right now, ob-viously, but I don't know. He's hard to read."

"I know he is. I don't like that."

"Listen, one hundred percent certain, the kid didn't flip. They would not be sending him to Otisville if he flipped."

"We're talking about human behavior, Mr. Gedny. Nothing is one hundred percent certain. Don't assume they're idiots. Don't assume they wouldn't try to trick us."

"That's just it," says Gedny. "They're not idiots. No way in hell the kid's still walking around out here if he flipped. Second he goes he's *gone*, right? Disappeared. He would not be walking into my office. You flip federal, you don't end up in Otisville. No, he's kept his mouth shut."

"So far."

Gedny nods, his mouth full of octopus. "So far. I'm not too worried about him. He's a good kid. He's smart."

"What are they doing with his girlfriend?"

"They made a lot of noise about charging her as an accessory, but nothing ever happened. She told them she didn't know any-thing, and they didn't believe her, and they didn't care. She's free of it."

Uncle Blue watches the waiter climb the spiral staircase, several plates balanced on his arm.

"Here's your steak. The chef sends his apologies. He wanted

you to try these tonight, the shrimp. He wants your opinion on the sauce."

"Fine, thank you."

"Anything else I can bring you gentlemen?"

"Not right now. Thank you, Jeremy. Tell Victor I'll speak with him later." The waiter nods and departs. Uncle Blue cuts open the steak and inspects the color.

"Got it right this time?" asks Gedny.

"Perfect. You were saying?"

"Brogan. He's a good kid. He'll be all right."

"He's soft," says Uncle Blue, checking his watch. "He won't last long in there."

"He'll have to. Fed mandatory, that means one day off per month of good behavior. We're talking eighty-four days over seven years. Your boy's not coming out quick."

"No," says Uncle Blue.

"You're going to see him before he's gone?"

"Later tonight."

"A goodbye party, huh?" Gedny nods. "Where, at VelVet? That's a good time. I've heard about some of those parties."

"You won't be there, Mr. Gedny."

"I know, I'm just saying they sound like fun. What do I have to do to rate one of those VelVet specials? Aside from getting locked up for seven years."

Uncle Blue chews his steak in silence for a moment and washes it down with red wine. "Win more trials."

Gedny licks his lips. "Listen, they found six hundred and fifty g's in your boy's sofa cushion. They got every white junkie on the East Side saying Brogan's the sell. Game over. What am I going to do? It's U.S. Code; there's nothing to argue. Who do I argue with, the fucking grid? Seventy-eight to ninety-seven months, automatic. Judge says eight-four, so eighty-four's the number. I kept him out of stepback, kept him out in the world for a couple months extra. Other than that—"

"*They* kept him out of stepback. This worries me. When they convicted Maravai, they cuffed him in the courtroom and took him to the holding cell. Brogan gets to walk out the door. He's free before sentencing and after sentencing he's free until his report date. The Bureau of Prisons ordered him to report directly to the institution, correct? It seems very unusual to me."

"Not so unusual," says Gedny, pouring himself more wine. "It's pretty common, actually, for nonviolent offenders. Maravai—"

"It makes me suspicious, Mr. Gedny. It makes me think the DEA asked the judge for this time. It makes me think they are still trying to flip him. Every day he meets with a federal probation officer, yes? What do they discuss?"

The lawyer shrugs. "Nothing much. He's clocking in. They just want to make sure he's around. You know why Maravai got stepback? He's a black kid with a record. Brogan's never been charged with anything before. He's a nice-looking white boy and the judge liked him; the judge liked his dad. His dad's bar is his bail bond; that counts for a lot. I don't think the DEA had anything to do with it."

"They know more than you think, Mr. Gedny. They went straight to Brogan's sofa. They knew exactly where it was. If Brogan's telling the truth, he was touched."

Gedny points at the ceiling and then his ear with his index finger. "We need to take a little walk after dinner. Get our galoshes on and take a little stroll."

"The restaurant is clean."

Gedny forks a shrimp, carries it to his plate, cuts the tail off. "I'm sure it is. And I'm sure everyone thought the Ravenite was clean, too. But I'd still rather take a walk. It won't be a long walk—your theory was right." Gedny takes a bite of the shrimp and raises his eyebrows. "That's an excellent shrimp."

FOURTEEN

B Y THE TIME Slattery has shaken the snow from his long cashmere coat and hung it from a hook, a glass of whiskey sits waiting for him on the bar.

"Hey, Jody," he says, cheerful at last. He feels this is an important moment in his life: for the first time a bartender has recognized him coming in the door and poured his drink without waiting for an order. If she got the drink right, he thinks, I'll remember her in my will. God bless her soul, it's Jameson's.

"I've got to make a phone call," says Jakob, shuffling off to the back room, slapping his wet Yankees cap against his hip.

"It's a big one tonight," says Jody, leaning into the bar, a practiced motion that introduces her cleavage to the conversation: *Good evening*. "The first big one of the year." Behind her the bottled liquor glimmers seductively below wooden shelves stocked with glass jars. Each jar holds a dead bug: giant roaches, moths, stag beetles, and millipedes.

"That's a new one, isn't it?" Slattery asks, pointing.

Jody turns her head to look. Slattery takes advantage of the moment to stare at her breasts. They are good breasts. They make him happy.

"Which, the banana spider? Yeah, Linda caught him when she

was down in Florida. Looks like a tarantula, right? Hairy legs and all."

"It's nice. She did a nice job."

Jody faces front and smiles. "You're making me nervous, admiring the bugs. That's a bad sign, my friend."

Jody gets called down to the end of the bar, and Slattery checks the door. Monty will hate this place; it's not a Monty place at all. Most of the drinkers here are regulars, slow-speaking white men who come for the country music and pretty bartenders. A heavy black fly buzzes past Slattery's face, and he slaps at it halfheartedly.

The Bug Bar was uncool for ages, became a hip dive for a few months after a famous divorce lawyer was shot in the bathroom, is now uncool again. Sawdust covers the linoleum floor. In the rear of the room a bearded man wearing a camouflage jacket practices trick shots on a pool table surfaced in red felt, the felt nicked and gouged and beerstained. A group of college kids plays cricket with their own silver-finned darts. A television above the bar shows highlights from the night's basketball games. A fat-necked old man sits hunched over a blinking video poker game next to the bathroom door. Jerry Jeff Walker sings from the jukebox by the window:

It's up against the wall, redneck mothers,
Mother, who has raised her son so well (so what! so what!),
He's thirty-four and drinking in a honky-tonk,
Kicking hippies' asses and raising hell.

Slattery sometimes wishes he were a redneck. He doesn't know any rednecks: there's Tex on the trading floor, who's from Oklahoma, but Tex went to Harvard and Slattery is pretty sure that rules out Tex, even if he does chew plug tobacco and wear boot-cut Wranglers. The one-seventy-seven-pounder on Slattery's college wrestling team, Zeke something, was from deep-western Pennsylvania, the true backwoods. What was his last name? He wore a Cat Diesel Power cap and always said things like "Aw, come on now, Big Frank, you putting me on?" Slattery hated being called Big

Frank; he enjoyed slamming Zeke into the mat for the entire two hours of early morning practice. Zeke seemed to enjoy it even more; he wasn't a very good wrestler but he had a disturbingly high tolerance for pain. Maybe Zeke was a redneck, but Slattery doesn't want to be Zeke; he wants to be the redneck from the song, getting drunk in honky-tonks, kicking hippies' asses, going home in his pickup truck alongside a couple of good ol' girls with hyphenated first names. Rednecks have it made.

Jakob returns from the back room, Yankees cap brimmed low over his forehead. Slattery watches him walk directly in front of a dart player in mid-motion, oblivious to all danger. The dart player gestures to his friends and mimes hurling his dart at the back of Jakob's head. Slattery feels the familiar constriction in his bowels, the feel of a fight about to happen. He wants to shake Jakob for being such a constant unwitting provocation, wants to punch the dart player in the mouth for threatening Jakob. He narrows his eyes at the dart player but the kid ignores him. Slattery wonders, for the thousandth time, how Jakob survives daily life in the city.

Jakob seats himself on the stool next to Slattery. "It's unbelievable. My mother says, 'You shouldn't be out tonight. It's the worst storm of the year.' And I say, 'Mom, I'm actually twenty-six years old.'"

"So why are you calling her in the first place?" The fat fly has landed on the bar, and Slattery watches it rub its forelegs together, a tramp warming his palms above a garbage-can fire. He brings his fist down hard but the fly wings safely away.

"You know my mom. She says she can't fall asleep at night until I check in. You should hear these conversations. It's incredible. She'll say, 'Did you get the thing from the thing yet?' And I'll say, 'Yeah, Mom, I got it two weeks ago.' You know? I mean, what is that? The thing from the thing? She doesn't speak with real words, but I understand what she's saying."

Jody returns with a wink for Slattery. "This your little brother, Frank? He's a cutie."

"Don't waste your time on me," says Jakob. "I'm in the sixty-second percentile."

Jody nods, pouring beer into frosted glasses. "But that's probably because you don't work on Wall Street. The scale is skewed toward the money thing."

Jakob stares at her, then at Slattery. "Does everyone in the city know about this?"

"Not everyone," says Jody, setting the glasses of beer in front of them. "Just everyone in here." She sticks her tongue out at Slattery and retreats to the far side of the bar, to the older men who sit down there, silently waiting for her return.

"Great way to make friends," mutters Jakob, crossing his arms on the bar top and leaning forward to blow patterns in his beer's foam.

Slattery concentrates on Jody, particularly on her ass, presented in cut-off denims, white threads snaking down her thighs. "What do you think of her?"

"Of who? Of *whom*?"

"Of Jody," says Slattery. "The bartender. It's a blizzard outside and she's wearing Daisy Dukes. You think she's cute?"

Jakob squints at Jody, shrugs. "She's pretty. She's pretty, except her face—"

"She's pretty except her face?"

"Her face is kind of weird." The fly lands on Jakob's ear and Jakob jerks sideways, nearly falling from his bar stool.

"She's pretty except her face is kind of weird?"

"So, okay," says Jakob, righting himself on the stool. "She's pretty." He removes his wet hat, bends the brim, traces the NY insignia with his fingertips. "It's all subjective. One of the guys at school, this biology teacher, Terry—have you ever met Terry?"

"No."

"I think maybe you did. At my birthday party last year. Anyway, he really likes this girl. In a sort of—"

"A girl," says Slattery. "What do you mean, a student?"

"A student, yeah. A junior. What's weird is, I mean this girl is *sixteen*. Maybe seventeen, I don't know, but probably sixteen. But you have to see her. She's not really pretty, but she's—I don't know, she's got something."

"Uh-huh," says Slattery, watching the televised basketball players.

"I told him—I told Terry he ought to just forget about it, put her out of his mind, but he's thinking about the future, he's thinking long-term. It's a little scary, the way he talks about it. He's like, 'Five years from now, she'll be almost out of college. And I'll be thirty-one. Nothing wrong with that.'"

"Miami won again," says Slattery. He turns to look at Jakob. "You haven't fucked her yet, have you?"

Jakob's eyes go wide. "See, if you listened you'd know I was talking about Terry. Terry's the one—"

"Remember when Mr. Green got caught blowing Eddie Arabian in the bathroom stall? That shocked me. I had no idea Green was gay."

"You understand it's Terry we're talking about, right?" asks Jakob. "Not me?"

"Why Eddie Arabian? Of all the guys in the school, *Eddie Arabian*? The kid always smelled like tuna fish. Hey, look who's here."

Naturelle stands behind them, a wet overcoat folded over her arms. She shimmers in her silver dress. Slattery knows this dress, he has memorized this dress, he has stood in the shower and cursed this dress, the way the fabric slides over her hips, the way it wrinkles at the belly when she sits down.

"Francis Xavier Slattery." She kisses him on the cheek as he half rises from his stool. "Hey, Jakob," she says, kissing him too.

Slattery pulls a stool over for her and she sits between them, her knees brushing against theirs. "What are you guys up to?" she asks.

"Frank's been—" begins Jakob.

The fly swoops past and Slattery takes a swing at it with his open palm, nearly cracking Naturelle in the jaw.

"Easy, killer," she tells him, poking him in the gut.

"Frank's been checking out the bartender," says Jakob.

Naturelle looks down the bar at Jody, who is mixing a brandy sour. "Yeah? What's the verdict?"

"Guilty," says Slattery. "Of looking *good*."

Jakob and Naturelle smirk at each other and then she punches Slattery's leg. "She's just tits, Frank."

"Whatever," he says, eyeing Jody's denim shorts. "The girl is oozing sex appeal."

Naturelle takes Jakob's beer and sips from it. "She's oozing something."

Slattery grimaces and turns to look at Naturelle. "I've noticed if a woman has great tits, other women think she's a slut. Why is that?"

"I haven't really studied this issue."

Slattery thinks for a moment, clinking his empty glass against the brass bar rail. "Women are beyond comprehension. Like, okay, you want an example? Talking in the movies. Why do women always have to talk while you're watching a movie? Or how come if I want to just call and tell her where we're going for dinner, how come I can't get off the phone for twenty minutes? It's like a sickness. Why do women always cry after having sex? What's up with that?"

Naturelle and Jakob stare at Slattery for several seconds, eyebrows raised. Then they begin to laugh, violently, Jakob raising his hand to his mouth as beer sprays out, Naturelle holding the bar rail to keep from toppling over.

"What?" asks Slattery. "What?" He frowns. "I mean, not *all* the time, but sometimes, sometimes. Come on, like you never do?"

Naturelle, gasping for air, reaches out to tousle Slattery's hair. "You're just a sad fuck, Frank."

Jakob bursts into fresh laughter, slapping the side of his stool. "You were just demoted from the ninety-ninth percentile, buddy."

Slattery is angry at himself for sounding like a fool, and especially for sounding like a fool in sexual matters. That is Jakob's role. Jakob is the one who asked, when he was *nineteen*, "Where's the clitoris?" Slattery answered, "About an inch deep in the ass," and bit his lip hard as Jakob nodded thoughtfully. Or the time Jakob asked,

"Don't you think a vagina looks like an alien's mouth?" Slattery tormented Jakob about that comment for months, though when he thought about it he had to admit that a vagina did look like an alien's mouth—or gills, anyway, something not human. Slattery made the mistake of sharing this thought with Monty, who shook his head and said, "What about the anus, Frank? You like the anus better?" Nobody could make Slattery feel like a fool faster than Monty, and Slattery suspects that nobody makes Jakob feel more foolish than Slattery. That was the way it worked among the three of them, from ninth grade on. Little fish gobbled by big fish gobbled by bigger fish—until now, when the biggest fish of all is about to swallow Monty whole.

More than anything, Slattery doesn't want Naturelle to think he's a fool. It's not that he wants to steal Monty's woman, he just wants to fuck her, one time. For years he has been subjected to her body, in a bikini at Jones Beach, in torn jeans in downtown bars, in black bicycle shorts in Central Park, in tight dresses in dance clubs. When Naturelle dances, Slattery tries not to watch.

One time he was playing basketball with Monty in Riverside Park. Slattery has always been a proud athlete; he does not enjoy sports he has no talent for. Still, he played hard that day, jogging to his spot under the net after each change of possession, grimly elbowing anyone who stood too close. All the men were shirtless, playing or waiting on the sidelines for the next game. The women stood on the perimeter of the court, fingers locked in the chain-link fence, chattering over the drumbeat of bouncing balls and skidding shoes. Naturelle wore a skirt so short that Slattery wondered why bother with a skirt. "That skirt's out of hand," he said to Monty. "I can see the bottom part of her ass." Monty just shrugged. "I can see your belly button," he said, pointing, and Slattery stared down at his outie.

Naturelle takes another drink from Jakob's beer. "What are you thinking, Frank?"

Slattery cracks his thumb knuckle. "Just wondering where the man is."

"Like he's ever on time?"

"He better be on time tomorrow," says Slattery. "If you don't show up when they tell you to show up, it's a felony."

The fly hovers near Naturelle's face; she purses her lips and blows it away. "He will. It's his dad's bar otherwise."

"How's his dad doing?" asks Jakob.

"He looks like he's aged twenty years the last few months."

"I always liked him," says Jakob. "He was always really nice to me. God, he's had it hard."

Naturelle nods. "This is a horrible thing to say, but I don't think Mr. Brogan's going to make it seven years. He has nothing left."

Slattery knocks three times on the seat of the bar stool. "Look, what are we doing? Sitting around talking about how sad it all is, what's the point? It's reality. Our boy's got ten hours left; what are we going to do, sit around crying, holding hands?"

Naturelle rises from her stool and smooths down her dress. "All right. Give us some more sex tips, that'll cheer things up. Which way is the bathroom?"

"Very funny," says Slattery.

"All the way back," says Jakob. They watch her walk past the dart players, who elbow each other and laugh as their leader mimes taking a dagger to the heart. Good-looking women are uncommon in the Bug Bar.

"I bet *she* cries after doing it," says Slattery, staring intently at the dart players, who resolutely ignore him. He raises his empty glass to Jody again, but Jody is watching someone enter the bar. Without turning around he knows that Monty is here at last. Women are always watching Monty enter rooms.

Jakob and Slattery rise and take turns embracing him. Monty's face is flushed from the cold, his watch cap and camel's-hair coat dusted with snow. His arms around his friends' shoulders, he smiles at Jody and orders three Jameson's.

"Nat's in the bathroom," says Slattery.

Monty nods. "You been here long?"

"Nah."

"They're throwing me a party at VelVet. We ought to go over there pretty soon." Monty releases his friends and scans the faces in the barroom. "What is this place?"

"Frank wants to be a redneck," says Jakob. "He comes here and whistles Dixie while he's peeing."

Jody lines up three glasses of whiskey. "You guys ought to come by on Sunday for the Super Bowl. We're setting up a big-screen TV. Linda has a cousin who plays for the Packers. He looks just like her, except he's six hundred pounds."

Slattery rubs the calluses on his palm and Jakob stares silently at the floor.

Jody laughs. "You don't have to come. I was just saying."

Monty claps his hands together loudly. Everyone stares at him. He takes a cocktail napkin from the bar and wipes the crushed fly off his palm, then balls the napkin and tosses it into the wastepaper basket below the cash register. He smiles and lifts his glass to Jody. "Fuck Sunday," he says, by way of a toast, and drinks his whiskey down.

FIFTEEN

T HE WHOLE CITY came out to say goodbye," says Monty, stepping out of the taxicab.

A roiling mob occupies the block, hundreds of teenagers camped out before the massive red doors of VelVet. Clots of smokers lean against the building, sheltering their lit cigarettes from the falling snow, cupping their palms to block the wind. Others sit on parked cars, drinking beer from forty-ounce bottles in brown paper bags. None of them are dressed properly for the weather, and none of them seem to care.

"You've got a lot of young fans," says Naturelle. "I think we're the oldest ones here."

"Wait here a minute," says Monty, and he slips through the maze of bodies and faces, boys and girls semi-engaged in languid, broken conversations.

"Tosh is having people over, but it's Tosh. . . ."

"I know. I hate that look. She's always giving me that look. . . ."

". . . already six inches. Seb's talking about boarding upstate tomorrow. . . ."

"I bought the first one. That's more jungle. He's not so jungle anymore. . . ."

"That's good green. That is good green. . . ."

"The R train is hell, man. It's like pioneer days. I'm riding that shit for weeks before I get home. . . ."

Monty makes his way to the velvet ropes. A pillar of a man wearing the exact same camel's-hair coat as Monty is checking names off a clipboard.

"Nice coat, you bastard," says Monty.

The bouncer frowns, looks up, and breaks into a broad smile. "It's the man. The man has arrived. Wearing my coat."

"No, no, no," says Monty. "My coat. I bought this two years ago."

"What's that, the Woolworth's special? It came with a set of flat-ware?"

"Khari, my young Negro friend, this is a Paul Stuart coat. Maybe you heard of Paul Stuart. That's the store you can't get into 'cause they take one look at your polyester-blended ass and laugh you back to Queens."

Khari smiles. "I hope you got some seven-year mothballs for that Paul Stuart coat."

Monty hesitates and then laughs, deciding it's better this way; he's sick of being around people who treat him as if he'll die in the morning. "What's with all the kids?"

"I've been seeing some serious fake IDs," says Khari. "This one punk had it perfect, New York State license, everything legitimate but for one thing; it said he was born in 1947. I look at him and I'm like, 'Buddy, no way you are fifty years old.' And he just says, 'Goddamn, every time. The fucker got the numbers reversed.' It was supposed to say 1974."

"What's going on tonight?"

"The legendary D. J. Dusk is spinning wax. My homeboy from Hollis. Boy's seventeen years old. He gets the girlies moving. But yo, they got the VIP room set up for y'all."

"I've got my people waiting on the street. You want me to bring them through here?"

"Nah," says Khari. "Bring 'em over to the avenue entrance. You know where I'm talking about?" He flips the walkie-talkie and catches it in his giant palm. "I'll tell them you're coming."

"Thanks, Khari."

"You got it. When you going in?"

"Noon."

"Otisville, right?"

Monty nods.

"Uncle got any people in there?"

"No one worth knowing," says Monty.

"My boy Etienne's at Otisville. Remember this name: Etienne Michaux. He's got sway in there. You going to remember that name?"

"Etienne Michaux. What is he, Haitian?"

"Nah, he's from Paris. Tell him you're friends with Khari. He'll set you up. He's in tight with the screws."

"The screws?"

"The guards, man, the guards. The federals, they run a nicer place. Lot nicer than State."

Monty smiles. "I'm a lucky kid."

"Luck of the Irish, right?"

"Luck of the Irish."

Khari grips Monty's shoulder. "Listen up—don't lose your temper unless it's time to lose your temper. You hear?"

"All right," says Monty. "I'll see you around the way." He slides back through the crowd and signals his friends to follow him.

Jakob steps onto the sidewalk and maps out his route. He watches disdainfully as Slattery lowers his head and bulls forward, forcing the youngsters to step aside as he crashes through them. No style, thinks Jakob. The tragedy of it all, he decides, is that nobody appreciates my one great talent. He cannot remember ever receiving a compliment for his pedestrian maneuvers. Tonight the level of difficulty is considerable: four drinks (six if you count the two with LoBianco), a packed sidewalk, slippery snow that makes lateral movement problematic. Monty is a good walker; Jakob can admit that. Monty is elegant. But it's obvious that Monty never really thinks about his walk; it's all instinctive. Naturelle drafts on Slattery; she lets him break through the mob and then follows him down the cleared path as the teenage boys turn to look at her. Jakob paces carefully after them, circling behind a stoned, swaying girl who holds her mouth open to the sky and tries to catch snowflakes.

"Hey, Elinsky! Mr. Elinsky! Hey!"

Jakob freezes for a second. Nothing good can possibly come of this. He keeps walking.

"Elinsky! Ha, it's Elinsky!"

A hand catches his sleeve and Jakob is forced to turn around, forced to stare into the unnaturally shining eyes of Mary D'Annunzio.

Jakob says, "Oh." He comes very close to saying Oh, no, but closes his mouth before the *no* can escape.

"What are you doing here? God, I didn't know you ever left the school. I thought you had a bed down in the boiler room or something."

Jakob's mind rifles through possible escape plans. He considers using *I am not who you think I am; I am the twin brother of Jakob Elinsky*—but the last time he tried that line nobody believed him and he ended up in worse straits.

"Mary D'Annunzio," he says, stalling for time. She wears a pair of old-fashioned dark denim jeans, the cuffs rolled up over her black boots; a fake raccoon-fur coat; and no hat, her wet black hair snaking across her forehead and neck. Black trails of eye shadow stain her cheeks.

"Mary B-plus D'Annunzio, that's me." She misreads the look of terror on his face and adds, "I'm kidding, it's not a big deal. It was kind of a crappy story, actually."

"I've got to go," says Jakob. "I'm here with friends."

"Yeah, that guy who was talking to the bouncer, right? He knows people, huh? What do you think, could he get us in?"

"Um, I don't—"

"They're not letting anybody in right now; they say it's too crowded already. I have to get in there. You're a fan of Dusk?"

"Sure."

"He's the absolute truth, right? He is so truth. I can't believe you're into Dusk! No offense, I mean, but I thought you were more into flutes or—"

"I think Dusk is very good," says Jakob, "but I like his earlier stuff better."

"His earlier stuff?"

"Jake, what are you doing?" Monty has circled back and now motions for Jakob to hurry up. "I've got a guy holding the door for us."

"I'm Mary D'Annunzio," she says, not letting go of Jakob's coat sleeve.

"Great," says Monty. "Come on, buddy, let's go."

"I'm with Jake," says Mary, resting her head on Jakob's chest. "We're lovers."

Jakob closes his eyes.

Monty grins. "Is that right? I didn't realize you two were lovers. Well, come on, plenty of room inside."

"Wait," says Mary. "I've got three friends."

Monty stares at her. "You've got three friends? What are you, retarded? You want to get in or not?"

"All right," she says. "Better one than none."

Jakob's eyes are still closed.

"Let's go," Monty tells her. "Get your lover moving and follow me."

"They'll catch up," says Naturelle, leading Slattery up a flight of stairs.

"You know where you're going?" Slattery carries both their overcoats draped over one arm.

"I've been here too many times," she says. "But they play good music."

Slattery commands himself to keep his eyes on the stairs and off of Naturelle's silver-clad behind. On the third flight of stairs he disobeys his orders for a moment, and then he is lost, everything in the world falling away from the beautiful shimmer before his eyes.

"Monty's acting strange," says Naturelle.

"Yeah."

"We've got to keep an eye on him. Okay? Frank?" She turns around and stares down at him. He looks up at her and smiles. "Are you listening to me?"

"Keep an eye on him. Right. Why, what are you thinking?"

She shrugs and continues climbing. "He's just acting really strange. You don't think he's acting strange?"

"He's going to prison in a few hours, Nat. How do you want him to act?"

"I want him to act like he's scared." She leads Slattery through a gray steel door and the music washes over them, a wave of bass. They stand on a long balcony fifty feet above the dance floor; they grip the railing and stare down at the writhing mass of people.

"I've never seen it this crowded," says Naturelle. Slattery shakes his head, unable to understand her over the music. "Here!" she shouts. "This way!"

He follows her to the end of the balcony, down a short flight of stairs. A man with a terrible burn scar across one side of his face, the skin unnaturally taut and glistening with ointment, stands in front of a velvet curtain. He smiles as they approach, bends down to kiss Naturelle's cheek.

"Where's the man?!" he asks, shouting into her ear.

"He'll be here in a minute! Oscar, this is Frank!"

Slattery and the bouncer nod at each other. Naturelle pushes aside the curtain and leads the way into the empty VIP room. "I guess we've got the place to ourselves. It's a little quieter, anyway."

"What happened to his face?" Slattery whispers.

"I don't know. I asked Monty and he says, 'He burned himself.'" She shakes her head. "It's like, Thank you, Montgomery."

Slattery hates nightclubs. He hates the ultra-hip kids who weigh ninety pounds and smoke unfiltered cigarettes, hates the bathroom scene where men stand for ten minutes before the mirror, pomading their hair, inspecting their smiles, adjusting the crotch of their pants. And, looking around, he hates this VIP room.

The walls are covered with crushed red velvet. The couches are upholstered in red velvet, the overstuffed chairs are upholstered in red velvet, the carpet is red faux-velvet. A small bar in the far corner is wrapped in red velvet. A pale woman in a green dress stands behind the bar, waving to Naturelle. A black steel question mark hangs from the ceiling in the center of the room, the period dangling seven feet from the ground. D. J. Dusk's pulsing beats pour from speakers bolted to the walls.

"Don't look at me," says Naturelle. "I had nothing to do with this."

"Get me a drink," says Slattery. He sits down on one of the chairs and closes his eyes. He has been awake since five-thirty in the morning. This night will never end.

"So how do you know Jake?" Mary asks, following Monty up the stairs. Jakob is in the rear. He is still not sure what is happening.

"We went to school together," says Monty.

"Really? Campbell-Sawyer? You went to Campbell-Sawyer? You don't seem the type."

"They didn't think so either."

"I hate that place. Elin—Jake's okay, but mostly it's—"

Monty stops and turns around. "How old are you?"

"Twenty-one," says Mary, no hesitation. "I was held back for a while."

"How old are you?"

"Seventeen."

Monty smiles. "Mr. Elinsky here, he's your teacher?"

"Yep." Mary turns and pats Jakob's arm. "I'm his best student."

"Look," says Jakob, "she's seventeen. We can't take her in here."

"Why not?" asks Monty. "We're already in."

"What's the problem? I've got ID."

"You're going to get people in trouble," says Jakob. "You could get the club closed down."

Monty snorts and begins climbing the stairs again. "Fuck the club. What did you say your name was? Mary D'Agostino?"

"D'Annunzio."

"What do you think of Mr. Elinsky?"

"He's all right." She turns and grins at Jakob. "He acts like a little old man sometimes."

"That's true, he does. I think tonight should be a big night for Mr. Elinsky. I think we should make sure Mr. Elinsky has fun for once."

"Okay," says Mary. "So when you went to C-S it was all boys, huh?"

Monty opens the fire door and leads them out onto the balcony. "All boys," he says, but the noise devours his words.

"Oh, listen to that! Listen! Dusk is so truth! We have to dance!"

"Not yet," says Monty. "We've got a party to go to." They can't hear him over the music but they follow him down to the VIP room, where Monty shakes hands with Oscar.

"I'll let people know you're here!" shouts Oscar.

"Give me an hour! I'm not ready for the whole deal yet!"

Inside Naturelle is seated at the red velvet bar, talking to the bartender in the green dress. They both turn to look at Monty when he enters. He raises his fists like a boxing champion, then slaps Slattery on the side of the head.

"Wake up, boy! What are you doing?"

Slattery opens his eyes. "I'm up. This room, I feel like I've been swallowed by a whale. What's happening?"

"What's happening? My farewell party is about to begin. Daphne! Champagne! Come over here and join us. D'Annunzio, this is Slattery."

"Hey," says Mary. She sits on the edge of the nearest sofa and looks around. "I've seen photographs of this room," she says. "The Smashing Pumpkins were in here." She stares at Monty. "Who are you? Are you somebody famous?"

Monty nods. "Do us a favor, D'Annunzio. Don't talk too much."

Daphne, the bartender in the green dress, walks over with two bottles of champagne in an ice bucket, followed by Naturelle, who carries a tray of flute glasses. Monty kisses Daphne on the cheek, draws one of the dripping bottles from the bucket, and begins opening it.

"Where's the bathroom?" asks Slattery, rising from his chair. The bathroom door is pointed out to him and he heads in that direction. "If the toilet seat is covered in red velvet, I'm hurting someone."

Daphne rests the ice bucket on a black steel table and returns to the bar. Monty pops the cork, spilling some champagne on the red carpet. He presses the bottle against his forehead, feels a vein pulsing against the cold glass. When he realizes that everyone's watching him, he grins and pours the champagne, hands out the glasses, and sits on the sofa. He motions for Jakob to join him.

"I need to dance," says Mary, shrugging out of her raccoon coat. She wears a white tank top with Tweety Bird emblazoned on the front. Tattooed roses garland her left wrist. She seizes Jakob's Yankees cap, her hands too fast for his dulled reflexes, and pulls it on backward. "Anyone want to dance?"

"I'll dance," says Naturelle. "You want to dance with us?" she asks Monty.

"A little later. Me and Jake need to talk."

"I'm Naturelle," she says, walking with Mary out of the room.

"I'm Mary D'Annunzio. I'm Jake's lover."

Jakob lies on his back next to Monty and covers his eyes with his forearm. "What are you doing to me?"

Monty grins. "She's cute, buddy. She talks too much but she's cute."

"You're going to get me fired. Do you realize that? She'll tell her friends, and they'll tell their friends, and pretty soon everyone in the school will know that Mary D'Annunzio and Mr. Elinsky went to a dance club together."

"So what, you went to a dance club. Tell them it was your friend's birthday and you got her in. You haven't done anything wrong, have you? Not yet."

Jakob sits up. "Yet? What does that mean?"

"You want this girl, don't you?"

"Shit, Monty, she's seventeen! She's my student. I can't touch her."

"I would," says Monty. "She's got that look. I like little girls with tattoos."

"Great."

"I don't see you much anymore. We've kind of gone our separate ways."

"I guess so."

"It's too bad. You're smarter than the people I know these days. Here," says Monty, raising his glass of champagne. "Make me a toast."

Jakob raises his glass. "You want me to make a toast?"

"Yeah. Come on, I won't be seeing you for a while. Say something nice."

Jakob stares at the tiny bubbles rising. "God, my mind's not working well."

"All right," says Monty. "Here's to Doyle."

"To Doyle? All right, to Doyle." They touch glasses and drink.

"He's your dog now," says Monty.

"What?"

Monty lets the champagne burn on his tongue for a moment before swallowing. "He needs a home. And he likes you."

"Yeah, but . . . I don't know. You've seen the size of my apartment."

"Poor Doyle, he'll be living in a small apartment. Hey, he's a tough dog. He'll get used to it."

"Why can't Nat take him?"

"She's moving in with her mom. Woman hates him. And Doyle doesn't like Frank. And my dad's allergic."

"What about Kostya?"

Monty runs his fingers across his scalp, silver rings plowing through his black hair. "Kostya won't be around. So that's it. There's no one else I can ask."

"I don't know," says Jakob.

Monty refills his glass. "They went all out for me, huh? Cristal. I'm a lucky guy to work with such caring people."

"One more glass of this and I'm officially drunk."

"Listen," says Monty. "This is important to me. Doyle is important to me. He's not a pet for me; he's a friend. I know what that sounds like. I know, it sounds weird. But listen, when I found him he wouldn't trust anyone. Anyone tried to pet him he'd bite their hand off. I found him and he was mostly dead, a couple hours more and the rats would have eaten him. The guys that used to own him, they put their cigarettes out on him, they beat him with chains or something. And he got his ear bit off in a dog fight."

"Yeah, you told me."

"Doyle is the toughest guy I know. He was lying there off the highway when I found him, and he was waiting to die. He knew he was going to die. And he didn't make a sound. He just sat there and said Fuck you to the pain, he said Fuck you to dying, he said Fuck you to me when I came and tried to help him. But I did, I helped him. You know that? You know that Doyle is the best thing I've done in my life? Think about it. It's the truth. The best thing I ever did, my whole life, was rescue that black little son-of-a-bitch. Every day he's had since then is because of me. Every time he runs through the park, that's me. Every squirrel he chases, every bitch he humps, every bone he chews—because of me. I saved him. And it's different than what you'd expect, right? Because it's not Doyle that's grateful. Nah, Doyle loves me but he doesn't remember any of that. What's weird is I'm the one that's grateful. Because I see him running around, I hear him barking, and there he is, the best thing I ever did, in the flesh. And I'm not going to let the pound have him. Doyle's the ugliest fucking dog in the five boroughs. Who's going to adopt him? Can you imagine, some mom and pop go in and pick him out and bring him back to their little daughter: Look, sweetie, a puppy for you! Can you imagine that, the kid screaming? Jesus, Doyle looks like he grew up in hell. And I'm telling you now, I will not let some vet stick a needle in him and end him. I saved his life, right? I'm responsible for him. I didn't go through all that just so some vet can put him to sleep. If it comes to that, I'll do it myself. I'll put a bullet in his ear tonight. So I'm asking you, Jake—for me, as a favor for me, and it's a big favor, but I'm asking you—will you take him? Will you take him home with you?"

Jakob is quiet, rubbing his palms over the red velvet sofa cushions. "You know what?" he says at last. "It would be an honor."

Monty smiles and there are tears in his eyes. "I was hoping you'd say that. I really was."

"Well, after that speech, Jesus Christ, how could I refuse?"

"Good," says Monty, beaming. "Now all we got to do is get you together with this D'Annunzio girl and your whole life will change."

"Hey, not funny. This is my student, Monty. It would be a very bad thing."

"Yeah," says Monty, resting his head against the back of the sofa and closing his eyes. "But so what?"

Slattery emerges from the bathroom and joins them on the sofa. "No more Chinese food," he says, rubbing his stomach. "Ever."

"Hey, okay," says Jakob, tapping Monty's shoulder. "I've got a question for you."

"What's that?"

"Do you think—"

"If you ask him if you look like a ferret," says Slattery, "I'm going to kill you."

Jakob pauses and then shakes his head. "I wasn't asking that."

"Who thinks you look like a ferret?" asks Monty.

"The kids at Campbell-Sawyer," says Slattery.

"No, they don't," says Jakob. "It's nothing. I wasn't asking that, anyway."

"Jake's been in a bad mood all night," says Slattery. "The boy needs some ass."

"The ass is out there on the dance floor," says Monty, eyes still closed, tapping the sofa cushions in time to D. J. Dusk's rhythms. Strange, ominous music, the accelerating drumbeat countered by synthesized organs. At times the theme seems ready to melt into dissonance, as if Dusk were threatening his audience with the possibility of chaos—but then he mutes the drums for a moment and the organ's lonely hum makes everyone in the club prick up their ears.

"What do you think, Frank?" asks Monty, opening his eyes. "She looks pretty good, right?"

"Who, the little one? Who is that girl?"

"She's my student," says Jakob. "Understand? My student."

"Is she the one that called you a ferret?" asks Slattery.

The lights go off and Monty half rises from the sofa, reaching for the gun holstered at the small of his back.

The lights come on again. Kostya is standing by the velvet curtains, his hand on the light switch. "The party begins without me?"

Monty releases the grip of his pistol and stands up. "I should have shot you, you fat Russian fuck."

Kostya ambles over, wagging his finger. "Ukrainian. Fat Ukrainian fuck." He bear-hugs Monty and kisses his cheeks. Monty stands stiffly in the big man's embrace. After he is released he wipes his face with the sleeve of his black sweater.

"Montgomery. My friend. You have been here long? And you open champagne without me? Frank! Hello, Frank!"

"Hi, Konstantine."

"Kostya. Please, Kostya. I am good, yes. Well"—he rests his meaty palm on Monty's shoulder—"I will be better when my friend comes back to us. Yes, hello. It is Jason, yes?"

"Jakob," says Jakob. They've met at least five times before. Jakob doesn't like Kostya. The Ukrainian is too big, too loud. Jakob doesn't like his silk shirts, his gold rings, his tobacco-stained smile. Kostya's front teeth are gone; he wears a bridge that he removes whenever he's drunk in order to leer at women and spit peanuts across the room.

"I have everything set up for you," Kostya tells Monty. He winks. "A very nice girl for you."

"I'm not in the mood."

"Ah, when you see her, you will be in the mood. I pick her out special for you."

"The last girl you picked out special had three teeth."

Kostya laughs loudly. "Funny you should say that." Everyone waits for the rest.

Finally Monty asks, "Why is it funny I should say that?"

Kostya shrugs. "It was funny, what you said."

Silence. "Wait," says Monty. "When you say, 'Funny you should say that,' it's like saying, 'That reminds me of this other funny story.' "

"No, no, I am saying what you say was funny. 'Funny you should say that.' You see? It was funny that you say that."

Nobody speaks for a moment.

"Come," says Kostya, at last. "You want to meet her?"

"I don't think so. Naturelle's dancing downstairs."

"So we go quick, we go right now. Yes? You must see this girl, Monty. I pick her out special for you. The champagne is good?"

"How many girls you get? You have someone nice for my friends?"

"Not for me," says Slattery. "Thanks."

Monty reaches for Slattery's hand. "Come down there with me. I need to talk to you."

"That's not my style, Monty. I really—"

"No, that's cool. I just want to ask you something."

Slattery grips Monty's hand and pulls himself to his feet. "All right. Lead on."

Jakob shifts uncomfortably in his seat. "Do you want me to stay here?"

"You've got to stay here. Who's going to look after Mary D'Agostino when she gets back?"

"Should I tell Nat you're downstairs having sex with a prostitute?"

"No," says Kostya, horrified. "Don't tell her that."

Monty smiles. "Tell her whatever you want. But don't take off—we'll go back to my place and get Doyle after the party."

Jakob watches the three men leave the room. Three men, he thinks. All of them have physical power, a presence; you walk into a room with these men and you feel secure, protected. Jakob always expected to grow *up*. His father is tall; his older brother rowed for Syracuse. Even his kid sister is an inch taller. What kind of man is shorter than his kid sister?

What does D'Annunzio look like when she dances? Jakob wonders. Is she dancing with a boy or with Naturelle? Mary D'Annunzio and Naturelle Rosario dancing together. That's an image to keep you warm on a winter's night. Jesus Christ, they're an orgy of vowels.

What must a man never ask in a Victoria's Secret shop? And who the hell is LoBianco to be moralizing? And where is LoBianco now? Did he make it home safely, or is he curled up and snoring in the corner of some Christopher Street old men's bar? Old and queer and out of work. Happy New Year.

The three men stand at the railing and look down at the dancers below. D. J. Dusk mans his turntables from a platform raised above the dance floor. He stands in the eye of an amber spotlight, flanked by sound monitors and generators that blow clouds of white smoke; he deftly flips a needle onto a spinning record's groove, and a burst of Keith Jarrett piano rises over an industrial backbeat.

"Look at her!" Kostya yells to Monty, pointing. "In black tank top! Swedish, you think? I never fucked woman with blond bush! Have you? Ah, look who I ask!" He elbows Slattery and winks. "Mr. Puerto Rico over here!"

"Why don't you shut your mouth," says Monty.

Kostya can't hear him, but he sees the expression on Monty's face. "I offend you? I apologize, my friend! Do not be angry with me!"

"Where's this girl you're taking me to meet?"

"Down in the Blue Room! You ready? I go make sure she's there. You like this girl! This girl is very nice!"

"All right, I'll be down in a minute."

"You go down there, you fuck her, you come back up and drink with your friends! That is party!"

"In a minute."

Kostya pats him on the back and walks away. Monty looks at Slattery, follows his friend's gaze down to a corner of the dance floor, and spots Naturelle and Mary in a cluster of sweating dancers.

"She looks good in silver," says Monty, just loud enough for his friend to hear. "Don't you think?"

Slattery stands straight as if poked from behind. "Who, Nat?"

"She's beautiful. She's the only woman—I've told you this, right?—Naturelle is the only woman I fantasize about after sleeping with her. I still do. Sometimes I'm riding in the subway and all I can think about is getting home and getting her naked. That's pretty normal, I guess."

"I guess," says Slattery. "Pretty good kind of normal."

Monty watches her. She has great confidence on the dance floor. She moves well, and she knows she moves well; the music skips beats and changes rhythms but Naturelle is never thrown.

"How's work going?"

Slattery shakes his head and points at his ear. Monty repeats the question, louder.

Slattery nods. "Work is good. This morning was big, very big." He waits to see if Monty will ask but Monty does not ask, so Slattery says, "I brought in two million dollars in about nine minutes. That's pretty close to a record. Not too many twenty-seven-year-olds are playing with that kind of money."

Monty watches as a shirtless, muscular white man, his arms sleeved with tattoos, crowds his way into Naturelle's circle and begins dancing with her. "So how much of that do you see?"

"What do you mean, like a commission? There is no commission; that's not the way it operates."

"So two million for them means zero for you?" The shirtless man has bent close to Naturelle to say something to her. She shrugs and spins away.

"It's all about the bonus," says Slattery. "The more money I make for the bank, the more I make for myself. We have this system now called capitalism. I don't know, I think it might work."

Two young men walk toward them on the balcony. When they see Monty they clap him on the back and shout in his ear. Both wear expensive suits without ties, thick gold chains glittering below their open shirt collars. Slattery watches the dancers. Now the tattooed man is speaking to Mary. Mary grabs hold of his belt and begins gyrating her hips into his pelvis.

"Six more months," says Monty, after his friends have left.

"Speak up!" Slattery hollers, and Monty nods.

"Six more months and I would've come to you, said, Here, here's the loot, what do I do with it? Let you play with it. Buy some stocks, kick back. Watched the coin multiply. Six more months. I got greedy. That's what happened. I got greedy and then I got fucked."

"You can't think about that stuff."

"Yeah, I can. That's all I *can* do is think about that stuff. I'll tell you what, Frank," says Monty, his voice calm and steady. Slattery has to bend closer to hear him. "I'm not going to make it. I always thought I was a tough guy, always thought I could take anyone, but it's a joke. I'm not going to make it. There's a thousand guys harder than me inside that place, and they're going to use me up and end me. Look at me! I'm a pretty white boy. I will not survive seven years in there."

"Yes, you will. You've got to."

"You're not listening to me."

"You don't have a choice, Monty."

"What?"

"I said you don't have a choice!"

"I have a choice. If I choose not to go in there tomorrow, I will not go in there tomorrow."

Slattery nods. "You're not running, though. If you wanted to run you'd already be gone."

"I'm not running," says Monty. "There's another way out."

"That's stupid talk," says Slattery, shaking his head. "You've got to be strong—"

"Strong? It's over, brother, finished. Strong for what? What do you want me to do, bite my lip when they start in on me? Don't tell me strong. Don't stand there like you know what to do."

"You're smarter than all of them," says Slattery. "Listen: you are. One week and you'll have the place figured, you'll know the names, the scenario. Just—"

"Let me explain the first night to you. Picture this, all right? First night, the place is overcrowded, they've got bunk beds set up in the gym to handle the overflow. You with me? Next thing I know all the guards are out of the room, they're laughing as they leave, looking at me and shaking their heads. *White boy, you are miles from home.* Boom, I'm down on the floor, someone big's got his knee in my back. I'm trying to get away, but there's too many of them. One guy starts smacking me in the face with a pipe. He knocks out my teeth; I'm choking on my own blood. They're kicking me in the ribs and I throw up, and there's teeth in there, I see my teeth in a puddle on the floor. They knock them out, they knock them all out. You know why? So I can give them head all night long and they won't have to worry about me biting. They'll make me a suck puppet for every yard queen in the house. And what if I make it the whole way through, what if I make it seven years, minus eighty-four days for good behavior? Then what? I'll be thirty-four years old when I get out. What kind of job am I going to get? What skills will I have? I'll be a punked-out convict with government-issue dentures. What the fuck is the point? I've studied this, Frank, believe me. I've looked at the options."

"Thirty-four is still young. Listen to me, would you? Hey, listen to me. You're still going to be a young man. I'll be set up by then; I'll be running my own place. You and me, we'll start something up. No, come on, hear me out. I'll be working, Monty, seven years I'm working. I'll work harder than every Ivy League fucker down there. And when you get out . . . we'll start something up.

I'll buy a restaurant, or a bar on the Upper West Side. There's big money in a good bar. I'll put in the cash, you'll run the place, we'll own that neighborhood. Couple of Irish kids from Brooklyn, Jesus, how can we not have a bar? Green beer for St. Paddy's Day, free hot dogs for Monday Night Football. Shit, one night a week I'll work the door, I haven't done that since college. Think about it. Old-fashioned jukebox sitting in the corner, pool table in the back—"

"Frank, can I tell you something? I appreciate this, okay? But I don't see a future in it. I don't see us working together. I don't see me and Jake hanging out. I don't see me and Naturelle. I don't see it."

"I didn't mention them," says Slattery softly. Monty is not looking at him, he shows no sign of having heard, so Slattery speaks louder. "I never mentioned Jake. I never mentioned Naturelle."

"Just you, huh?"

"Tell me something, okay? Have I ever broken a promise to you? Have I ever once in my life broken a promise to you? Have I ever said I would be somewhere and not shown up?"

Monty is quiet for a moment, staring at his hands. "No."

"I'm telling you I will be there and I will be there."

"Okay," says Monty. "But you're not going to be there tomorrow."

Slattery nods and says nothing.

"So I've got a favor to ask you. You're my brother, right, my best friend?"

"You know that."

"I need you to do something for me."

Slattery waits.

"Not here," says Monty. "We can't do it here. Can you come uptown with me and Jake? I'm giving him Doyle."

Slattery smiles. "I was afraid you were giving me the dog."

"Nah, Doyle can't stand you. We'll leave here in a little bit. I'll meet you back in the VIP room, okay? I've got to say goodbye to some people. Sound good?"

"Whatever you want," says Slattery. "You know that."

"Good." Monty returns his eyes to the dancers. The shirtless man is lying on the floor, curled up on his side, his hands between his legs. Mary and Naturelle are nowhere in sight. "Our friend Jake," says Monty, "has picked himself a winner."

SIXTEEN

J AKOB STARES AT the black steel question mark and sips from his
glass of champagne. He wants to be home, stretched out in his
warm bed. He has been awake for too long.

The red room is growing crowded. Jakob does not recognize
any of them pushing through the velvet curtain, these loud-
speaking men holding champagne flutes in ringed fists, lean
women who stand in clusters, heads bowed together, murmuring
in low tones. Jakob sits alone on the sofa and eavesdrops, tries to
fish phrases from crosscurrents of accent: Brooklyn, New Jersey,
Boston, Dominican, Eastern European, Puerto Rican, Brazilian.
He hears the name Monty spoken in four different languages, a
dozen dialects, but always the same hush descending, the way
friends sitting shivah mention the departed.

Jakob wonders how many would gather for his own farewell
party; he compares the imagined group to the crowd before him
and feels a sharp pain at the smallness of his life. Who would come?
A bunch of English teachers in chalk-stained blazers; Paul from the
math department; Slattery; two or three college friends who would
huddle around the whitefish and swap good Jakob stories for eight
minutes, exhausting all the good Jakob stories. Monty's existence
seems impossibly dramatic, guns and prostitutes and South Ameri-

cans, a life worth hearing about. If someone wrote the history of us, Jakob thinks, if someone decided to tell the story, where would I be?

The room is hazy now with cigarette smoke. D. J. Dusk lays down a heavy bossa nova beat, Elis Regina calling out one phrase in a looped sample. Three women in the center of the room drop their purses on the floor and dance around them, vigilant and abandoned all at once. Jakob imagines strolling out to join them, their skeptical looks fading into stunned admiration as he swings his hips in a provocative manner, drops into a perfect split, begins walking on his hands. He frowns. I can't even imagine myself dancing well, he thinks angrily. I'm picturing a gymnastics routine. He drinks the last of his champagne, tries to stand, is not successful. Oh, boy, he thinks, I'm drunk.

He dips his head against the sofa's velvet armrest and closes his eyes. Don't drop the glass, he tells himself, his last coherent thought before the fuzz of dream logic occupies his mind. Don't spill the milk.

The next thing he senses is the pressure of a warm body curled up alongside him, a hand unwrapping his fingers from the champagne flute's stem. Somewhere deep down in his consciousness an alarm rings, a muted bell clanging *danger!* But the red velvet is too comfortable, the heavy heart-thump of bass too embryonic, too lulling, everything too warm.

He feels fingernails following the curves of his ribs and some part of him knows the name that goes with these fingernails; another part of him knows that this is what he wants—these nails, this warm body. The name and the want never collide but skitter around the edges of his mind like repellent electrons.

But then a tongue curls along the inside of his ear and he hears his own name whispered by a voice he cannot render anonymous. *Jakey,* comes the whisper. *Jakey.*

He keeps his eyes closed for another moment and wishes the whisperer into a dream, but she doesn't fade away; her tongue, nails, and voice linger on him. He opens his eyes and sees Mary D'Annunzio straddling him, a knee on either side of his lap, her hazel eyes peering at him from below his Yankees cap. A strong urge comes over him to damn the rules and regulations, but he remembers himself, with an unpleasant start, in time.

"Whoa, what are you doing? Mary, get off me."

Mary shrugs and falls onto her back on the red velvet cushions, her black Doc Martens still resting on Jakob's thighs. "Don't panic. Nobody here gives a shit."

"I give a shit," he tells her, shoving her feet off him. "What do you mean, nobody gives a shit? Do you know what happens if somebody sees me—us—like that?"

He observes that it's true, though; nobody in the room seems to have noticed them. The three women still dance around their purses; the men still argue loudly, gesturing with their cigarettes; Daphne still maneuvers through the thick of it with her tray of cocktails.

Mary, lying on her back with her feet dangling off the edge of the sofa, is also examining the crowd. "You know what? I've got a feeling the Campbell-Sawyer faculty don't spend much time in the VelVet VIP room."

Jakob sits up straight, rolls his shirtsleeves down to his wrists, buttons them. "I'm here, right? You never know."

"I just kicked some guy in the balls. He's on the ground throwing up."

"Did you? That's nice." Jakob leans forward and rubs his temples with his thumbs. "Mary?"

"What?"

"Why did you kick some guy in the balls?"

She grins at the memory. "I was dancing with him and he decides to put his hand down my pants. He had his hand like inside my ass. So what was I going to do?"

The terse description of a stranger's hand inside her pants becomes an irritatingly vivid image in Jakob's mind. He tries to block it but cannot; he sees thick fingers slipping under the dark denim waistband and grabbing the white curves beneath.

"He's rolling around on the floor saying he's going to kill me, describing how he's going to kill me, so Naturelle went and got a bouncer and they threw him out. Naturelle's in tight with the bouncers. She's cool as shit. I love that name, right? Na-tur-elle! One hundred percent Naturelle. Naturelle flavors!"

"Yeah, the great thing, she's never heard those jokes before. You could really entertain her." He stares at Mary's chest. Tweety Bird stares back, alarmed.

"So what's up with her boyfriend? It's like he owns this place."

"Listen, Mary, do you think it would be possible to avoid talking about tonight at school?"

"I think it would be possible."

"That would be a really good thing," says Jakob. "I think it would be really smart for both of us."

"You think it would be possible to give me an A for the term?"

Jakob stares at her bruise-painted eyelids, her lank black hair. "Tell me you're joking."

"I'm joking, Mister Elinsky. You know my favorite word in the English language? Swoon. I love that word. Swoon. I've never swooned. I'd like to, you know. Just sort of swoon and somebody pretty would catch me."

"Right. So we're agreed, no talking about tonight?"

Mary smiles and closes her eyes. "That's what I like about you, Elinsky."

"What's what you like about me?"

Mary opens her eyes. "I can't remember. What was I talking about?"

"Never mind."

"Dusk is for real. Isn't he? Hello? Elinsky? Do you think I'm weird?"

"No," says Jakob. "I think you like to play around sometimes, but you're not weird. You're . . ." Jakob closes his mouth before the outlaw word—*beautiful*—can escape. "Not weird."

"Deering thinks I'm weird. My mom thinks I'm weird. That's why they have me in Ruben's office all the time. They think I'm weird."

"Dr. Ruben talks to a lot of kids."

"Yeah, and they're all weird. They don't send normal kids to the psychologist's office."

Conversations I Never Wanted to Have, thinks Jakob, number 9307. "Well—"

"Jenny Klemperer is bulimic, Ian Hart never showers, Sebastien McCoy talks to himself, really loudly. Freaks. *Weir-does*," she sings.

"Jenny Klemperer is bulimic?"

"Jenny Klemperer is bulimic and she's still fat. That's *really* weird. I mean, what's the point?"

"Okay, actually, let's not do this, please. Let's not talk about them."

"Yeah, but I think she wants people to talk about her. Which is kind of weird right there."

"You don't want people talking about you?"

"If it was good things, sure. But, I mean, why would I want someone saying, Look, there's Mary D'Annunzio, she pukes in the toilet after lunch every day. That's not the reputation I'm gunning for. Hey, you coming to see *Hamlet* next week?"

"Of course. You're in it, right? Ophelia?"

Mary rolls her eyes. "Fuck Ophelia. Laertes."

"Laertes?"

"You want to see my death scene?" She springs up from the sofa and takes three steps back, then begins staggering toward Jakob, hands folded over her gut. " 'Exchange forgiveness with me, noble Hamlet: Mine and my father's death come not upon thee, nor thine on me!' " She collapses onto the red cushions and quivers there, moaning.

A group of men smoking cigars in the corner clap loudly. Jakob scowls at their grinning conference and realizes he is jealous. Other men shouldn't be looking at the girl I'm with, he thinks, even if she is my student. They don't know she's my student.

Jakob stares down at the prone Mary, at the stretch of pale skin between the dark denim waistband of her jeans and the white cotton of her tank top. A row of three vertebrae calls out for a finger to connect the dots. Jakob wants to cover her with a blanket or else peel the clothes off her body.

Mary sits up and brushes her black hair away from her eyes. "It's better with the fake blood."

"No, it was very good. You have a fan club."

"Ms. Taylor says I'm the best dier she's ever had. Did you see *Romeo and Juliet* last year? I was Mercutio. That was the greatest death of all time. My mother cried. My mother cries at everything, but still. You know what I'd really like to be? A stuntwoman. Except I'm afraid of heights. You think they'd hire a stuntwoman who was afraid of heights?"

"I don't know. Maybe." Jakob wishes he didn't sound so boring, but he is half convinced that he ought to sound boring, that any interesting comments would constitute flirtation.

"I actually need to leave about now," he tells her. "And I think you should probably leave too."

"You really want to be seen leaving a dance club with me?"

He hadn't thought of that. "All right, you leave first and I'll leave a little later."

"Screw that," says Mary. "Dusk only plays New York a couple of times a year. He's huge in London. I'm not walking out until the sun is shining. Anyway, tomorrow's a snow day for sure."

Jakob rubs his eyes with his palms. "I need to go to sleep."

Mary lies back and kicks her feet into the air, begins a bicycling motion with her hands behind her head. The rolled cuffs of her baggy jeans fall to her knees and Jakob stares at her slender calves, at the tattoo of braided lilies that encircles her right ankle. How many tattoos does she have?

"Can't sleep yet," she says, bicycling madly. "He's turning it on."

Jakob nods. He finds himself strangely entranced by the music, the lush, humid tropicality of it, a drumbeat incantation, Regina's one phrase a mantra, a snatch of words Jakob cannot translate sung in a tone that makes translation unimportant.

"You know what I love about you, Elinsky?" Mary asks, nudging his hip with her foot. "The way you walk. It's like you're planning everything out, left foot here, right foot there. It's like the way you hold a book. You're standing up there teaching and you're holding this book—Melville or whatever—you hold it like it's something fragile, this baby bird; if you squeezed too hard you'd kill it. I love that. I have to pee."

Jakob watches her make her way through the crowd, stopping to dance for a moment with the three women in the center of the room. He watches a tough-looking man with slicked-back hair appraise her, then turn to his friends and nod. He watches her grab Daphne's wrist and stand on tiptoe to whisper something into the taller woman's ear; he sees Daphne smile and hand Mary a blue drink. He watches her open the bathroom door and disappear inside, and he knows it's over; he knows he's lost. He stands and walks unsteadily to the far side of the room; he leans against the red velvet wallpaper and waits for the bathroom door to open.

A minute later it does and Mary is staring up (staring *up*! he notes happily) into Jakob's face, her eyes as wide as Tweety Bird's.

"You need to pee?" she asks.

"No," says Jakob. He presses forward, backing her up, and closes the door behind him. The bathroom is black-walled and lit by a single blue bulb.

"Hi?" asks Mary, her teeth glowing in the eerie light, and Jakob grabs her by the shoulders and kisses her hard on the mouth. It's a great and guilty kiss, a blue kiss, a shock of a kiss. Jakob's toes curl upward; his eyelids stay closed long after the kiss is done. It seems necessary that his hands move to her breasts, and they do, fingers pressed to the underwire of her bra.

Blame it on the champagne, he tells himself, a thousand little bubbles rising through my veins, aerating my brain. Good, she's very good, soft where she should be soft and firm where she should be firm. Blame it on the champagne. Champagne for my real friends, real pain for my sham friends.

Only now does Jakob realize that she's not kissing him back, that her tongue is still, her hands open and lax by her side. He jerks away from her, wiping his mouth with the back of his fist. The Yankees cap sits crookedly on her head. She stares at the floor and Jakob's mouth is open; he turns around and rams through the bathroom door, shoves past cigar smokers and dancing women; he's running now. He pushes through the velvet curtain and runs.

SEVENTEEN

THE WOMEN MONTY knew growing up were loud, cursed bois-
terously, and gnawed on chicken bones. Not like the fragile girls
he met from Manhattan's prep schools, who looked ready to shat-
ter if you yelled at them, to lie inert and crystalline on the hardwood floors of their duplex apartments. Naturelle was just right, a
neighborhood girl who could play the uptown game.

He met her in the playground of Carl Schurz Park, two blocks
from her high school, on a hot September afternoon. She and a
friend were sitting on the swings, smoking cigarettes, when Monty
walked past, holding a dripping cone of vanilla soft-serve with
chocolate jimmies. He was twenty years old. He had just sold fifty
decks of black tar to an Englishman for two thousand dollars. The
Englishman could have bought the same amount for five hundred
dollars if he had walked two miles uptown, but he didn't know
he was overspending or else he didn't want to explore the streets
of Harlem, and either way Monty's silver money clip was now
jammed with hundreds.

Monty sat on a green park bench and licked his ice-cream cone,
watching the two girls swing higher and higher. They wore their
school uniforms: white blouses embroidered with the school's ini-
tials and green plaid skirts over black tights. Monty wondered if

the black tights were part of the dress code; he thought they were a bad idea. As the girls kicked forward, legs held straight in front, all he could see beneath their skirts was black, a censor's blot hiding all the fun.

They knew he was watching them and they knew they looked good, their athletic legs straight, then bent, straight, then bent, their long hair falling beneath them as they kicked higher. Monty gave the blonde high marks for her long thighs, but he focused on the brunette. While the blonde kept her cigarette clenched in one hand as she started swinging high, the brunette never stopped taking reckless drags, the crook of her elbow holding the chain lightly as she soared skyward. Her disdain for the danger thrilled Monty; he expected her to fly off the edge of her seat at any second, fly off over the East River to land with a bang in Queens. But she didn't; she swung and smoked and chatted with her friend, all of it effortless, a gentle pumping of the legs.

A little boy cried as his mother dragged him by the wrist away from the slides. The sandboxes were filled with children building a skyscraper, a bucketful of sand balanced on top of another bucketful of sand on top of another, up and up, until the whole thing collapsed and the kids screamed and laughed and started again. The bigger boys played dodge ball in a sunken court where the sprinklers sprayed during the summer.

Monty swallowed the last of his cone and wiped his lips with a paper napkin. He walked over to the girls and sat on the free swing. Puerto Rican, he decided, watching the brunette. A scholarship girl. She whizzed by him on the way to the top of her arc.

"Hey," he said, "could I bum a smoke?"

She whizzed by again. "What?"

"A smoke," said Monty. He thought asking the girl for a cigarette would force her to stop for a minute, but it didn't.

"This is my last one," she told him, whizzing by.

"You go to Chapin, right?"

"Yeah."

"You know a girl named Ella Butterfield?"

The blonde braked with her feet and skidded to a halt. "I've met you before, haven't I?"

Monty nodded, though he was sure he had never seen the girl before in his life. "Yeah, I thought you looked familiar. Are you friends with Ella Butterfield?"

"I know who you are. Come on, Nat, we've got practice."

"You know who I am?" asked Monty. The brunette began slowing down, watching him. "Who am I?"

But the blonde said nothing. She jumped off her swing, picked up her bookbag, and walked away without looking to see if her friend was following.

Monty turned to the brunette. "So you're Natalie?"

"Naturelle."

"Really? Naturelle. I like that. Naturelle. So what's your friend's problem?"

"You're the one who got thrown out of Campbell-Sawyer for knifing some guy during a basketball game, right?"

Monty laughed. "Now I knifed him. No, that's not why I got kicked out. How come you didn't follow Blondie to practice?"

She shrugged. "I want to finish my cigarette."

"Where you from, anyway?"

"The Bronx."

"Yeah, I figured you were F.A. What's your name?"

"How do you know I'm F.A.? How do you know I'm not from Riverdale?"

"Because the only Puerto Ricans in Riverdale are there to wax the floors."

She flicked her burning butt over the fence, stood up, and began walking away.

Monty jumped off his swing and chased after her. "Wait, hey, hey, I'm sorry. I'm insulting *Riverdale*, not Puerto Ricans. I was F.A. too."

"Go away."

"I'm not insulting you; it's a neighborhood thing. Hey, come on, I'm sorry. I can make it up to you. Dinner anywhere you want, you pick the place. Come on, at least look at me. You're kind of mean-looking when you want to be, you know that? You look a little like that guy on *Sesame Street*, what's his name? The Cookie Bandit. You look like the Cookie Bandit. Hey, talk to me, Cookie Bandit. Come on, I said I was sorry."

"Cookie Monster."

"Right! Cookie Monster. You're smart too. So come on, you talking to me again? Are we friends again?"

"You're too old to be hanging out in playgrounds," she told him, and left him standing there.

"All right," said Monty. "Same time tomorrow?"

Not the smoothest first meeting, he thought, but Monty was blessed with cockiness—he was sure the girl liked him despite all signs to the contrary. So he borrowed Ella Butterfield's yearbook, found the only Naturelle and her last name, and began leaving gifts for her with the school's receptionist. Platinum bracelet, pair of amber earrings, chinchilla vest: one a week, the receptionist now a grinning co-conspirator. Naturelle accepted the gifts but never phoned the number prominently written on every accompanying note after the first line, which always read: *Give me a chance.* Finally Monty hit on inspiration: he left her a single Knicks ticket, court-side seat, first home game of the season.

That night he wore his brand-new midnight-blue suit and a wildly expensive pair of Italian suede cap-toe boots, carefully slicked his hair back from his widow's peak, arranged his silver rings, and surveyed the crowd at Madison Square Garden. I own this town, he told himself. Someday I'll own this team and make myself the starting point guard. He winked at the usher and walked down the concrete steps to courtside. One of his seats was occupied by a fat man in an orange T-shirt sipping Coca-Cola through a straw.

"Time to go," said Monty. "Let's go, out."

"Fuck you," said the fat man. "This is my seat." He waved his ticket at Monty.

"Where the fuck did you get that?"

"My sister. She told me to say hi, and she's sorry she couldn't make it tonight. She's waxing floors in Riverdale."

Monty grinned and sat down. "Let me buy you a beer."

The next ticket Monty left for Naturelle was to a modern dance recital at the Brooklyn Academy of Music. His note read: *Tell Hector the curtain goes up at eight sharp and they won't let him in after that. And tell him not to wear the orange shirt. He got mustard stains all over it.* And at five to eight, in the lucky borough of Brooklyn, Naturelle Rosario walked down the aisle and took her seat next to Montgomery Brogan.

In VelVet, early in the morning of the last Friday in January, Monty watches as a pretty woman unzips his fly and slowly runs a long fingernail along the underside of his cock.

"What's your name?" he asks her.

"Maggie."

"Maggie, huh? I like that. Maggie."

"Short for Marguerite," she tells him, smiling.

She is kneeling now on the blue cushions and Monty shuts his eyes, gives himself over to her skill, to the undeniable solace of a good blow job. Behind closed eyes he is stripping the clothes off Naturelle: the black tights, the green plaid skirt, the white blouse. He is running his hands down the smooth swell of her flanks, gripping her to him, this body he knows so well, the smell of it, the taste of it. Then it begins to break down. His hands are on the slick Naugahyde of the sofa, not Naturelle's skin. The smell in the air is from old cigarettes and spilled alcohol. He opens his eyes and stares at the blue walls and when he tries to imagine Naturelle again her face is blurred, refusing to take form. He feels himself weakening in Marguerite's mouth even as she bobs her head with increased vigor, doing her best to stimulate him. He shuts his eyes again and tries to will Naturelle into life but it's not working. Naturelle is gone from his mind; now he is traveling north through the cold countryside, on the long bus ride to Otisville. Monty has never lived anywhere but the city; he has never left for more than a week.

He counts the telephone poles, the depressed little towns that line the highway, the snow-covered fields.

Finally he taps Marguerite gently on the shoulders and she backs away from him, looking up at his face for a moment before blinking and licking her lips.

"It's my fault," he says. "You're very beautiful."

"You're very handsome," says Maggie, after taking a long swallow of champagne. "Are you an actor?"

"Yeah," says Monty, zipping his fly. "I'm a star."

When the woman leaves he raises his glass of champagne to his eye, turning the blue walls green. Somewhere in this city children are screaming and nobody can hear them. Somewhere in this city a fire is burning and nobody is there to put it out, no wonderful fireman to douse the flames.

EIGHTEEN

NATURELLE FINDS SLATTERY sitting at a bar in a tucked-away corner of the club, hunched over his whiskey, a blue handkerchief pressed against his face with one hand, his black cashmere coat draped over the neighboring stool. The room is meant to look like the library of an English country manor: dark wood paneling, walls lined with bookshelves filled with old leather-bound books, flickering sconce lights mimicking gas lamps. Two men with dreadlocks sit facing each other over a chessboard in the middle of the room; one taps his queen's crown thoughtfully while his friend shakes his long hair back and forth in time to D. J. Dusk's beat.

"Francis Xavier," says Naturelle, squeezing the back of his neck, "what kind of party is this?"

Slattery wipes the handkerchief over his eyes, folds it, stuffs it in his pocket. He sits up and smiles at her, his eyes red, and Naturelle feels a shock of guilt. Before this moment she could not have imagined Slattery crying.

"Hey," he says. "Saw you dancing before."

"Why are you all alone?" She sits on the stool next to him and touches his shoulder. "Are you okay?"

He nods. "I couldn't sit in that goddamn red room anymore.

It's a mob scene. I don't know any of them. These are Monty's friends?"

"I guess so. They're around a lot, anyway."

Slattery nods and tilts his glass, watching the whiskey lap up against the rim. Each time he turns his wrist the whiskey seems sure to spill over, but it never does. Naturelle stares at the rolling whiskey, mesmerized, until Slattery puts the glass to his lips and finishes it.

"I hate this place," he says. "That's the gap between me and your man. I hate places like this and he loves them. Also, he's better looking."

She laughs. "Now you're getting all Irish, drinking whiskey and feeling sorry for yourself. Have you seen him around?"

"Wasn't he dancing with you?" Slattery checks his watch and curses. "I'm supposed to be at work in an hour. Jesus, I can't even imagine working today. You just gave me the flu, okay? I'm calling in sick."

"I wish Monty could call in sick," she says, looking at Slattery's empty glass. "Where is he?"

"He's around somewhere. He's probably saying goodbye to all the bouncers. And the manager, what's his name? Saying his good-byes." Slattery turns to check on the chess players. "I've been sitting here for forty-five minutes and that guy still hasn't moved."

Naturelle smiles. "Haven't you noticed something strange about that game?"

"He ought to center his rooks, for one thing. They're no use to him sitting in the corners."

She jabs him in the ribs with her finger. "All the pieces are black, Frank."

Slattery blinks and then widens his eyes. "What are they doing? They're both playing black? Who went first?"

"I don't know. I guess it doesn't matter. They're all on the same side."

"So what's the game?" asks Slattery. "Where's the fun? The bishops fondle the pawns?"

"Listen, I wanted to ask you, can you do me a favor?"

"What's that?"

"Keep an eye on Monty, would you? Try to stick with him tonight. He's making me nervous."

Slattery turns away from the chess game and studies Naturelle's face. "What happened?"

"Monty's not Monty right now. This is killing him, the waiting. I don't think he really understands fear, you know? I think this is the first time in his life he's scared, and he doesn't get it; he doesn't know what's happening."

Slattery shakes his head. "He's been scared before. How old was he when his mother got sick, seven? He told me he didn't sleep the whole time she was in the hospital. You know how long she was in the hospital?"

"Three months."

"This is all so stupid," says Slattery, the blood coming to his face. "It's so stupid. He's got so much going on, he's so smart, and what does he do? He throws it all away. And here I am, his supposed best friend—I mean, right? I'm his best friend?"

"He loves you, Frank. You know that."

"His best friend, and what do I do to stop it? Nothing. Never a word. When he started selling pot to kids in Campbell-Sawyer, did I say anything? When everyone's talking about buying from Monty, the whole school, and I knew they were going to nail him, *knew it*, did I say a word? The last ten years, I watch him get deeper and deeper, and these friends of his, these fucks you wouldn't want petting your dog, did I say, *Hey, Monty. Careful now. Get out of this*? Nothing, not a word. His best friend. Goddamn, Naturelle, I'm his best friend and I just sat there and watched him ruin his life. And you did too. Both of us, all of us, we just sat there and let him."

Naturelle runs a fingernail down her forearm and inspects the faint white trail. "Monty never listens. You know that; you know how stubborn he is. I told him he should quit a hundred times—"

"Did you? Was that before or after moving into his apartment?"

She knows the signs of a Slattery periodical: the slitted eyelids, the thick-knuckled fingers twitching. Still, she's always been able to calm him before. "Don't start," she says quietly, touching his knee. "Not tonight, Frank."

"Was that before or after he gave you those diamond earrings? Or let you drive his Corvette around town so you wouldn't have to carry shopping bags on the subway? Were you confused about where that money was coming from? What paid for those earrings, Nat? The two of you fly down to San Juan—hey, great time, introduce him to your grandmother—did you pay for the tickets? First class all the way, right? What paid for Puerto Rico? You told him to quit? The hell you told him to quit. Come on, that whole bullshit story about how he got you to go out with him, the gifts, the courtside seats—what paid for it? You knew then what he was, everyone in every private school in Manhattan knew what he was. You didn't complain then, did you? You've never had a real job in your life. You've been living off the fat, Naturelle, and you never said a goddamn word."

Naturelle stares at him, her nostrils flared. "Who are you to get all righteous with me? Did you disown him? You're his best friend and you never said a thing, but this is *my* fault? I'm the evil one?"

"I never took his money."

"How long have you been saving this? One minute ago I thought you were my friend. I sat down thinking, There's Frank, my friend, I want to talk to him. Are you drunk, Frank? Tell me you're drunk. Tell me you're sorry, you've been drinking too much, you don't know what you're saying."

"I know exactly what I'm saying. Seven years from now I'll be waiting at the gate and you'll be married to money."

"Frank, what is wrong with you? You want me to be the bad guy? Okay, I'm the bad guy. You want to hit me now? Will that help? What do you want to do to me? What do you want, Frank?"

Slattery sits silent, his thick neck red.

Naturelle stands up and smooths the wrinkles in her silver dress. "When you see Monty, tell him I went home. Tell him I'm waiting for him there. And Frank? If you remember this conversation tomorrow, if you get the urge to send me flowers, or call up and apologize? Don't."

Slattery watches her walk away. He watches the dreadlocked men intent upon their impossible chess game. He watches his hands, sitting open on his lap, meaty-palmed, crook-fingered. This way is better, he tells himself. This way there won't be any temptations.

NINETEEN

IF YOU TRANSPORTED a man from the Middle Ages into this night-club, thinks Jakob, he would surely believe himself damned to hell, imprisoned among a swaying horde of ill-lit souls who wet the dance floor with their sweat, boys and girls and girls and boys, no couples, everyone dancing together or everyone dancing alone.

We are in hell, thinks Jakob. The great bad kiss has sobered him and given him an immediate hangover, his tongue dry and heavy, his stomach dyspeptic, his skull throbbing in time with D. J. Dusk's bass line. He needs to speak with someone, to confess his crime, to come up with a plan, but he's sure nobody here can help him. Slattery won't pay attention, or else will laugh and make a joke of it. Monty won't understand the problem. Naturelle? Naturelle will think I'm a pervert. And why should they care, anyway? They have more important things to worry about than a stupid, stupid kiss.

He asks a bouncer where the telephones are and the giant, never looking at Jakob, unfolds his arms, gestures vaguely with a long finger, refolds his arms. Jakob finally finds the phones in a narrow corridor across from the bathroom marked *XX*, a cute touch he would normally find aggravating but now scarcely notices. A line of women snakes out the door, most of them slouched against the wall, resting their feet and inspecting the ash on their cigarettes.

Jakob picks up the nearest phone and shudders as the receiver comes free in his hand, the chrome-encased wire dangling like a severed umbilical cord. He carefully replaces the receiver in its cradle and moves to the next phone, deposits two quarters, dials Brooklyn.

LoBianco picks up on the eleventh ring. The only man Jakob knows who has never bought an answering machine.

"Anthony? It's Jakob. Were you sleeping?"

"They're playing *Shane*. I must have seen this movie forty times, and it still gets me. Alan Ladd was a bit of a fattie, wasn't he? A bit of pork on him. Different times. Women used to like their men meaty. You know what I realize, watching this? Jack Palance is the real star. Look at those eyes. He looks more like a snake than a snake looks."

"I really need to talk with you."

"You *are* talking with me. That's what we're doing. We're talking."

Jakob looks at the line of women propped against the wall, exhausted suspects waiting to be fingered by a witness behind one-way glass. "I did something really stupid just now. Can you pay attention for a minute? Are you drunk?"

"What have you done?" asks LoBianco, perking up. "Have I inspired you? Have you crossed to the other side?"

"What?"

"Let me guess. It was a kiss."

Jakob drops his forehead onto the plastic partition separating the telephones. "Yes."

"Oh-ho, oh-ho, well, this is cause for celebration, my boy. I think I deserve a little credit, no? For my prod. My little push. Just a little push in the right direction. It's often that way. It's like jumping into the deep end; you need your father there, you need someone to goad you on. So who was this boy, mm? Where did you meet him?"

"What are you talking about? I kissed Mary D'Annunzio."

"Mary D'Annunzio?"

"I'm in a nightclub and I was drunk and she's drunk or stoned or whatever and . . . okay? I kissed her. I kissed Mary D'Annunzio."

"Who?"

"D'Annunzio! Jesus, Anthony, you taught her in the fall. Mary D'Annunzio!"

"The little raven-haired actress? Ah. Well, it's a roundabout way of getting there, but maybe that's best."

"Anthony, are you hearing me? I kissed a student of mine!"

"On the cheek? A chaste peck on the cheek?"

"Open mouth. And I might have touched her breast."

Jakob looks up and sees the line of waiting women intently listening to his conversation. A girl with red pigtails waggles her eyebrows. "Hubba hubba," she says.

"Anthony?" Jakob whispers into the phone, turning his back on the women.

"You're not supposed to do that, you know," says LoBianco.

"Yes, thank you, I'm aware of this."

"I wouldn't panic. She's not the type to rat you out. It would go against her whole ethos. She's a passionate little girl, she reads Guevara's *Guerrilla Warfare*, she won't blab to the authorities."

"That's . . . I don't know. I can't believe I did this."

"Give me a moment, the ice has melted."

Jakob peeks over his shoulder and the pigtailed girl grins at him. He buries his face in his shirt and listens to the sounds of gunfire coming over the telephone line.

"Still there, my boy? Ah, that's it for Palance. He was quick, though. He nicked Ladd with a forty-five, but Ladd's too much man for one bullet. Oops. Look what I've done. The thing about vodka, Jakob, the thing to remember: it never stains. There we go."

"So what should I do? Should I talk to her? Apologize? Pretend nothing happened?"

"Woman trouble. Always seemed like such a mess, that whole

field. My father was a great playboy, a great lover of women. And what did he ever get? My mother. And then me. Serves the bastard right."

Jakob bangs his head against the partition and waits, holding the receiver down by his hip. Finally he lifts the phone again and speaks with as much calm as he can muster. "Anthony, please."

"Say this for him, though: he was terrifically fertile. He couldn't unzip his fly without making somebody pregnant. According to neighborhood legend, illegitimate LoBiancos litter the five boroughs. I'm rumored to have a mulatto brother in Flatbush."

"Nobody uses the word mulatto anymore."

"No? Half-breed? Well, regardless, all that loving got him nowhere. He mounted one filly too many and that was the end of him. Something popped in his brain. Spent his last six months drooling while my mother sat in the corner, knitting. The greatest sweaters she ever made. There they were, drooling and knitting, Antonio in the bathroom masturbating. The All-American Family. Took Dad six months to get it right, to finish the job. He was a big man before. The bed used to look small with my father in it. But after the stroke the bed kept growing and growing, until it swallowed him up."

"I'm sorry," says Jakob. "I don't—"

"And then he was dead. A little dead man draped in a giant's skin. Six months after I die they'll come up with a cure for death. I read about it. They'll make you drink this goop, and in the goop are ten million robots the size of your cells. And the robots will go swarming through your body, destroying all the bad things. It's coming, Jakob. Death is a rotten idea and some bright boy will end it. They'll have to murder all the rabbits in the world, testing the goop. But if it's to save somebody's daughter, and it's always somebody's daughter, then fuck the rabbits. Let them grow thumbs and war on us."

"Listen—"

"I can't tell a story straight, can I? That's my problem. I hate straight stories. My father, my father, he's the star. One of his mistresses had the audacity to show up at our apartment, a few days before the end. My mother was very disturbed at how ugly she was. Oh, she had the face of a fiend. But everyone was very polite, and drank coffee, and watched Dad drool. And later Mother said, 'Can you blame the girl?' and I thought she meant, for being ugly. Of course I could. I blamed the ugly woman for being ugly, and the dying father for dying, and the kind-hearted mother for mothering. Everyone is equally responsible for the shit they bring into the world."

Jakob holds the receiver to his ear and says nothing.

"You understand, my boy? I can't help you. And you can't help me. Nobody can help anybody."

"I don't believe that."

"The trouble with this world," says LoBianco, "is it has nothing to do with what people believe."

Jakob's face grows hot; he feels the anger surging through his body and he welcomes it—a pure, clean anger burning away the complexities, the shame and self-loathing and fear.

"And the trouble with that philosophy," Jakob says, speaking very quietly but enunciating each word carefully, "is you end up by yourself, drinking bad vodka and watching late-night movies and not giving a shit about anyone."

"Yes. Well, that's true too."

"Good night, Anthony." Jakob hangs up the phone and walks away, the pigtailed girl whistling in his wake.

TWENTY

—

"S O?" ASKS KOSTYA, grinning. "You like her?"

"She's very nice," says Monty.

"Does she have three teeth? Eh? No, I think she has many teeth. I think you like her."

"I said so, didn't I? She's very nice."

Kostya nods. "Very nice. Come, Uncle wants to see you."

Monty follows the Ukrainian down the long, dimly lit corridor. It seems to him now that he is distant from this scene, that he is watching himself walk behind the glass of a static-ridden television. He watches, exhausted, as a pale-skinned actor playing Montgomery Brogan marches forward. And though he knows he ought to be afraid, Monty the watcher cannot summon any fear for Monty the actor.

He has not seen or spoken with Uncle Blue since the trial; his only source of information has been Kostya, who sugarcoats everything, and the lawyer Gedny. But nobody ever knows what goes on in Uncle Blue's mind.

Kostya knocks on a steel-plated door and turns to wink at Monty. A balding man smoking a cigarette opens the door and closes it behind him. He nods at the two of them and they hand him their pistols. Checking the safeties, he shoves the guns under his belt and then, cigarette clenched between his teeth, carefully pats them down. It occurs to Monty that he is not checking for weapons. When he has finished his search he raps on the door and it opens. Kostya and Monty enter the room. The balding man follows them inside, hands their guns to one of the Zakharov twins, and walks out of the room again, closing the door behind him.

They're posting a guard, thinks Monty. He knows that something is wrong, but he is too tired to think through the tangles. Only the thick pulse of the drumbeat can be heard down here: steady, distant cannon fire.

Monty has been in this room before, the club manager's office. He stares at the celebrity photographs on the wall and waits. Uncle Blue sits behind the desk reading a newspaper, the fingers of one hand combing through his black beard. Senka Valghobek sits on the front of the desk, smoking, heavy gut bulging beneath an unraveling diamond-patterned sweater—a sweater, he once told Monty, that his dead wife knit for him twenty years ago. Valghobek nods at the newcomers and smiles, flashing a broken front tooth, his eyes deep-set beneath a single brush stroke of eyebrow. He gestures at the black plastic chairs, and Monty and Kostya seat themselves. The redheaded Zakharov twins stand behind them; Monty has never been able to tell them apart. They were athletes in the old country, Red Army boxers, small but frighteningly fast. Monty gets along with them but he knows they despise Kostya, considering him a braggart and a liar. One of the twins takes the pistols over to Uncle Blue and places them carefully on the desk.

Uncle Blue folds his paper neatly. "Montgomery," he says. "How is the party?"

"It's all right," says Monty. "Thanks for setting it up."

"The first time I went to prison, I was fourteen years old, a skinny little boy. Very afraid. By the time I came out I had my beard; I was a grown man. I went back to my hometown, I found my mother, I kissed her. And she screamed." Uncle Blue smiles. "She did not recognize me. I have been in three different prisons,

Montgomery, in three different countries. You know what I learned?"

Monty shakes his head and waits.

"I learned that prison is not a good place to be."

Kostya laughs. "I knew that before I went."

"Nobody's talking to you," says Valghobek. "Keep your mouth shut."

"Seven years is a long time," says Uncle Blue. "Some men would do anything to avoid seven years in prison."

Monty waits.

"Your father's a hard-working man," says Valghobek. "Where's his bar? In Bay Ridge? Eighty-sixth Street and Sixth Avenue, am I right?"

"Yes," says Monty.

"At least he has a short commute," says Valghobek. "He can practically walk to work. Where does he live? Seventeenth Avenue? And what was the cross street? Eighty-first? Eight-oh-two Seventeenth Avenue. Is that right? The first floor. That must be noisy, living on the first floor. But he doesn't walk to work, does he? He drives. A 1987 Honda. Should I tell you how many miles he has on that car?"

Monty says nothing.

"Your father," says Uncle Blue. "I like your father. A hard-working man. He has had bad luck, some very bad luck. It made me sick what happened to your mother. Everyone in the neighborhood loved her. You remember her, Senka?"

"Sure. She was a beautiful woman. A real sweetheart."

"I want to help your father," says Uncle Blue. "I could use a man like that, a hard-working man, a man I could trust. He is very experienced, am I right? He could manage one of my clubs, make good money. I could take care of your father. Do you understand what I mean, Montgomery?"

Monty keeps his eyes on the floor and speaks very quietly. "You don't need to do this. I never said a word to anyone. You don't need to bring him up."

"I asked you a question, Montgomery."

"I understand exactly what you mean."

"I have a good job for your father," says Uncle Blue. "We'll help him with the money he owes. Maybe I'll buy the bar, put him to work on Third Avenue. What do you think?"

"He likes his bar."

"He likes his bar, good, we'll work something out."

Uncle Blue turns Monty's gun in his hands, judging its heft, checking the slide's action. He ejects the magazine, peers at the top cartridge, slaps the magazine back into the pistol's butt.

"Good weapon. Accurate?"

Monty nods.

"Polymer frame, very good, easy to clean. And reliable? No jams?"

Monty shakes his head. He feels a slithering in his bowels.

Uncle Blue smiles. "Have you ever fired it? At somebody, I mean?"

"No."

"No. Good. It is a toy for you. Not toy, prop. A prop for you. Like an actor. Am I wrong? With the gun you feel more . . . dangerous?"

"I never said a word to anyone. They came after me to get to you. I know it, you know it. They don't care about me. But I never said a word."

"I believe you," says Uncle Blue. "When you get there, Montgomery, figure out who is who. Find a man nobody is protecting, a man without people. And beat him until his eyes bleed. Let them think you are a little bit crazy, but respectful, too, respectful of the right men. You're a good-looking boy; it won't be easy for you. But remember, I was fourteen when I first went. And I survived." He nods and stares into Monty's eyes. "We do what we have to do to survive."

Uncle Blue points at Kostya, and the Zakharov twins grab the Ukrainian from behind and throw him to the floor. One of them jams his knee into Kostya's back; the other presses the muzzle of his pistol into Kostya's ear. They tell him something in Russian and the big man stays very still, his face mashed against the bare concrete floor.

Uncle Blue watches this activity before nodding at Monty again. "You should have told us before."

"Told you what?" asks Monty. He's not looking at Kostya. He doesn't want to see. He doesn't want to hear the man's frightened, ragged breathing.

Valghobek shakes his head and exhales smoke through his nostrils. "How many people knew you kept the stuff inside the sofa cushion? Eh? Your girlfriend, Kostya, who else? You must have figured this out before."

"Monty," moans Kostya, "please, Monty—"

The twin holding the automatic pulls back the slide, chambering a bullet, but Kostya keeps moaning anyway, "Monty, please, Monty—" until the other twin slams his face into the concrete, twice.

Monty closes his eyes.

"Kostya dimed you out, little brother," says Uncle Blue. "He made a call and stole seven years from your life."

"Of course he did."

Uncle Blue squints at Monty through the cloud of cigarette smoke. "You should have told us."

Monty opens his eyes and stares back. "You should have known it yourselves. You told me to trust the man, and I trusted the man, and now I'm gone seven. It took you this long to figure it out? They touched him, and he had two strikes so he touched me. Nothing very complicated about it."

"I don't understand you," says Valghobek. "This man, this whore, sells you federal and you don't care? You turn the other cheek? Why didn't you tell us?"

"Nobody asked me."

Uncle Blue waves away the smoke between their faces and leans closer. "Calling out a rat doesn't make you a rat. It's justice." He picks up Monty's gun and hands it to Valghobek, who carries it over to Monty.

"I don't want it."

"It's yours," says Uncle Blue. "You know how to use it?"

Valghobek holds the pistol by the barrel, waiting, a small smile on his face, until Monty grabs it from him and stands.

"I know how to use it."

"Good," says Uncle Blue. "This man does not deserve to live. He betrayed you, he betrayed me. He stole from you. He stole seven years from you. End him."

Everything seems stupid to Monty now, stupid men playing at stupid games, a confusion of menace, of treachery, all for such petty stakes. A fool's drama played by dim thugs reciting the same lines endless generations of dim thugs recited before.

The Zakharov twin holding the gun taps the muzzle against the back of Kostya's head, where the skull meets the spine. He grins up at Monty. "Right here," he says. "Very quick." He straightens up and backs away. His brother continues to hold Kostya down; he nods at Monty and watches him.

Monty crouches beside the Ukrainian and points his gun. Kostya struggles to turn his head. Blood leaks from his nose. "Monty—"

"Don't talk."

"Listen, Monty, please listen. I had no choice. I—"

"You had a choice," says Monty. He looks into his old friend's eyes and feels no pity, no pity for this man who drank vodka with him, played cards with him, who took him to Russian restaurants in Brighton Beach and taught him to curse in three languages.

It seems to Monty that revenge is the simplest of all pleasures, the most understandable: someone hurts you, you hurt them back. And won't it make things easier, seven years in a cage, knowing that the man who sent you there is not lying on the beach as the waves roll in, enjoying the summer sunshine; is not sitting in the raw bar at Grand Central Station slurping oysters from the shell; is not hollering at the hockey players to pass the puck; is *not*, period.

"It doesn't matter anymore," says Monty, flicking on the safety. "What's the point? I could have told you about Kostya seven months ago. It was too late then and it's too late now. You kill him, you bury him, I'm still going to Otisville. What's the point?" He tosses the automatic to Uncle Blue, who catches it and frowns.

"Be careful," says Uncle Blue.

"I'll be careful. And you be careful too. You think I'm soft, don't you? You think I'm soft?"

"Monty," says Valghobek. "You want to watch what you're saying."

"No, I don't. It doesn't matter to me. Not a goddamn thing matters to me, except this: if anything happens to my father, I'll kill you both."

One of the Zakharov twins asks a question in Russian, but Uncle Blue holds up his hand.

"Go ahead," says Monty. "You give him the order if that's what you want. But if I walk out of this room, we're done. You hear? I'm out, my father's out."

"It won't change anything," says Uncle Blue, gesturing at Kostya, who has begun to sob quietly on the floor. "You're not saving anybody."

"You want to let me go or not?"

Uncle Blue drums the desktop with his fingers. Valghobek lights a new cigarette, puts out the burning match with a flick of his wrist, and drops it on the floor. Everyone waits. The bass line is barely audible down here, but Monty can feel the vibrations in his bones. A glass of water sitting on the desk trembles slightly.

"Remember what I told you," says Uncle Blue. "A man with no friends."

He nods at Valghobek, who walks over to the door and opens it. Valghobek blows a perfect ring of smoke and Monty watches it rise, trembling, toward the fluorescent lights.

"Come on," says Valghobek. "You're missing your party."

TWENTY-ONE

THREE YOUNG MEN—silent and shivering in the underground station—sit with their backs against the corrugated steel shutters of a closed newspaper stand. Two teenage boys with shaved heads and sleepy faces stand at the far end of the platform, sipping from a carton of orange juice that they pass back and forth. One old man, wearing a black garbage bag with a hole cut out for his head, leans against a blue I-beam that helps support the station's ceiling. He holds a small radio close to his ear and listens to an evangelist preaching in Spanish. Snow is melting in the old man's hair; it drips down his neck, down the black plastic of the garbage bag, puddles at his feet.

Slattery hears the two boys laughing; he sees them crouched at the platform's edge, staring at the tracks. He leans forward but can't make out what they're laughing about. Monty and Jakob are paying no attention, but Slattery is curious, so he stands up, walks toward the boys, asks, "What's down there?" His breath rises in white vapors above their heads.

The boys examine him for a moment, reckon him safe, point. Slattery peers into the darkness. "What?" And then he sees the pink tail of a rat slip under a steel rail. His eyes begin to pick out movement in the shadows, and he counts six, seven, nine rats crawling in the tracks, nosing through balled-up paper bags, wax-paper cups, candy wrappers, orange peels.

"These ones," says the taller of the boys, "they eat rat poison like chocolate. The MTA keeps putting more and more poison down there, and the rats get fatter and fatter. People talking about getting snakes, these pythons from Africa, getting a bunch of them and letting them loose in the tunnels. To eat the rats."

"They should just get cats," says Slattery. "It would be cheaper."

The boy scowls. "Cats would get hit by trains. That's the thing, a snake could just slide under."

Slattery smiles, trying to imagine a New York politician importing African snakes for release in the subway tunnels.

"My uncle works for the MTA," says the boy. "He told me, one time, these guys were down here working on the tracks, and one guy felt something crawling up his leg, under his pants—and he starts screaming. By the time his friends get to him, the rat's chewing his balls off."

"Come on," says the short boy.

"It's true. That's why you see guys, nowadays, working down here in the tunnels—next time you see them, check it out—they all tuck their pants into their boots. I'm telling you," he says, over his friend's clucking.

"Watch this," says Slattery. He digs around in his pants pocket for a handful of change, picks out a nickel, and hurls it at the closest rat. The nickel flashes by the rat's head and clangs off the rail. The rat hustles into the dark alcove below the lip of the platform. A chorus of high-pitched squealing makes the boys laugh.

"They're saying, Look out!" says the tall boy.

"Here," says Slattery, offering a palmful of change. "Take a shot at it."

The boys look at each other for a moment and then each takes a coin. They stare up at Slattery. He nods at them.

"Let's see what you got."

The taller boy takes careful aim at a fat gray rat whose head and front paws are inside an empty bag of potato chips. He throws the coin too hard; it pings off the tile on the far side of the tunnel, below the red spray-painted tag: SANE SMITH.

"Your release is too high," says Slattery. "Look." He mimics the boy's motion. "See? You're letting go way up here, so it's floating on you. It's like—you play football?"

"No."

"Baseball?"

"No."

"No? What do you play?"

"Soccer."

"Soccer? All right, forget it. Your turn, little man."

The small boy hands the orange juice carton to his friend, crouches with one hand on his knee and the other, coin-holding hand resting on the back of his hip, like a pitcher on the mound, reading the catcher's signals. The fat gray rat now sits back on its haunches, gripping a sliver of potato chip between its paws. It takes a nibble and looks around, black eyes small and wet like two drops of blood. The boy raises his left leg high, in the manner of the great Juan Marichal, rears back, and fires sidearm. The coin spins through the air and they're all watching it—even the rat is looking up now, solemnly nibbling its fried potato—and *pthhwick*! the nickel smacks it on the head. It drops the chip, quivers for a moment, and bolts into the shadows, its brother rats squealing and the humans cheering.

"Thataboy!" yells Slattery. He raises his hand and the boy slaps it, grinning happily.

"You see that? You see that?" shouts the tall one. "Rat got clocked! Charlie got mad velocity!"

Charlie says nothing, just grins and hops around on one foot.

"Every now and then, fellas," says Slattery, "you got to show the rats who's boss."

Jakob watches the kids at the far end of the platform jumping up and down and wonders why they're so excited. He checks his watch. Six o'clock. Three hours until the bus leaves Port Authority headed north to Otisville. Monty sits next to him but he's not there; he's a cold space, unspeaking, unblinking, hunkered down in his camel's-hair coat, staring at a gray concrete floor freckled with tramped-down chewing gum.

When Slattery found Jakob sprawled on a black velvet chaise lounge in a back corner of the club, he helped him to his feet and said, simply, "Monty wants to go home." None of them said a word on the long march to the train station. Jakob kept looking back at the six rows of footprints that trailed behind them, slowly filling with new snow.

He knows he should say something to Monty now, do something, some gesture of solidarity, even an arm around the shoulders, anything, but he is stiff with fear, with exhaustion, with the sick memory of that kiss. He keeps seeing Mary D'Annunzio's face flattened with shock, her bewildered eyes, the Yankees cap sitting crooked on her head. It's not the sin of it that really bothers him, not the immorality of the situation, it's the rejection. A kiss that had his toes curling left her disgusted, her tongue retreating to the back of her mouth, her hands hanging limply by her side. How much better to be a winning lecher, a seducer, to corrupt young women and get run out of town! But to fail with the seduction, to have the girl step back, revolted, wanting nothing but to escape . . . ?

LoBianco is right about one thing, thinks Jakob. Mary won't go running to the headmaster. But she will tell her friends, won't she? Don't girlfriends discuss everything, every wart on their lover's anatomy? Imagining the conversations is horrifying for him. He pictures the girlfriends gathered about Mary in the coffee shop, twisting straws around their fingers, their mouths wide with the erotic thrill of good gossip. *He kissed you?* they would shout. *Oh, my God! He kissed you? What was it like?* Mary would shake her head. *Ugh*, she would say. *Awful. He slobbered all over me. Like kissing a ferret.* They would scream and laugh and ask, *What are you going to do? You could sue the school. Maybe they'll arrest him!*

If the kiss had been better, he thinks, if I had kissed her right, everything would be okay. Monty, if Monty had gone into that bathroom, wrapped his arms around her, laid on a Monty smooch, Jesus, the two of them would still be in there; there would be a line of ten thousand people with bursting bladders banging on the door.

What is worst of all for Montgomery, thinks Jakob, the worst possible punishment, is to be deprived of women, to be exiled to a stone city of hard men, scarred losers with razors in their pockets and a lifetime of defeat to avenge. Monty has always been comforted by women; they have always adored him, protected him, covered his face with kisses, gazed at him on the sidewalks. What disturbs Jakob is the quick twinge of justice he feels when he considers the situation. He has waited years for his turn. He remembers the interschool dance in tenth grade, when a pretty young cleft-chinned girl had walked bravely up to him and, looking over at Monty, asked, *Who's your friend?* Someday, he always told himself, the girls will look my way.

For the next seven years, thinks Jakob, I will live in a city gone mad with beautiful women, everywhere, waiting at the corners for the light to change, sitting in Bryant Park watching the outdoor movies, hanging onto the straps of swaying subway cars, serving drinks in Chelsea bars, jogging around the reservoir, yelling at their boyfriends on Avenue A, whispering into pay phones, smoking outside Indian restaurants, dancing in the dens of apartments that have dens. And Monty will wait in Otisville, watching a television bolted to the ceiling, the glass protected by a wire-mesh screen. He will sleep in a cell with strangers he cannot trust, he will use a bathroom where the walls are smeared with shit, he will eat food prepared by convicts, knowing the rumors about broken glass in the chili, maggots in the rice.

Jakob can imagine the prison, but he has no idea whether his picture matches the reality. The only prisons he knows are from television and movies: the fantasy penitentiaries where an innocent man fights to survive while at the same time proving his innocence; where an old lifer, sentenced decades ago, provides tactical advice on how to combat the gangs, the sadistic warden, the loneliness. Jakob sees the old lifer perfectly, the battered face still mournful for the wife he murdered in the fifties.

How does Monty imagine it? Does he understand what is happening to him? Jakob stares at him now and can't read a thing. Monty's green eyes are dulled over, like the eyes of a fish you wouldn't buy. Jakob wants to ask him what he sees right now, what he's picturing, if it's Otisville or Naturelle or how this all got started. But Jakob asks nothing; he rubs his hands together and shivers. A few more hours and I can lie down in my warm bed, between old flannel sheets. I can boil water for tea and sip it while watching the snow fall outside my window. They'll have to cancel school today. I can sleep late, wake up in the early afternoon, watch the cartoons, root for the cat to finally catch the mouse.

"Are we sure the train is running?" Jakob finally asks. Monty does not answer. He's not present. He's in a hospital on Seventh Avenue in Bay Ridge in 1977, visiting his mother.

She had begun to look like someone else, like something else, something monstrous pretending to be his beautiful mother. He didn't like this new woman, he hated her; she was trying to trick him, to make him believe she was his real mother when it was so obvious she couldn't be. She was an impostor. When she spoke it was nothing like his real mother; it was a rasp that almost never made it to the end of a sentence.

At home he had drawn a picture of two women, one with curly hair, one bald, and his father had asked who they were. "That's mommy," the boy had said, pointing to the curly-haired woman. He put a finger on the bald woman's face. "That's the robber mommy."

When his father told him they were going to the hospital, Monty cried and yelled until his father slapped him hard on the face. Monty stopped crying. He hated his father for thirty minutes but was holding his hand by the time they got to Seventh Avenue. Monty wore a plastic fireman's helmet, candy-apple red, with a sticker on the front that read NEW YORK CITY FIRE DEPARTMENT. They rode the elevator, and an old woman in a bathrobe, leaning on a walker, smiled at Monty and asked his father for a light.

When they got to the room Monty did not want to go in; he squeezed his eyes shut and covered his ears with his hands and shook his head violently. "Monty," his father said, uncovering his ears, "please. Help me out here." His father had never spoken to him like that before. Monty opened his eyes, took his father's hand, and followed him into the room.

The robber mommy looked at him and smiled; she reached out for his hand and drew him close. He was afraid but she drew him close. He didn't know what was happening but he knew it was bad. She held his hand and said, "Don't be scared."

"I'm not," he said.

"You look very handsome in your helmet," she told him.

"I'm going to be a fireman," he said, and she nodded.

"I know you are." She closed her eyes and a shudder ran down the length of her long body. And then another and then another. Her hand dropped Monty's and clawed at the bedsheets. Mr. Brogan gripped his son by the shoulders and led him to the doorway. As he left the room Monty heard his mother speak, with great effort. "You're going to be a wonderful fireman, Montgomery."

He did not turn around. He left his father behind, walked down the hospital corridor, his basketball shoes squeaking on the shining floor, and stopped at the open door of another room. An old man lay in his bed, tubes running up his nose, into his arm. A radio on the nightstand played opera. The old man saw Monty standing at the door and beckoned for him with one curling finger.

"*Figlio mio,*" said the old man. "*Dov' è il fuoco?*"

Monty ran. He ran so fast the fireman's helmet flew off his head, but he did not stop; he ran to the end of the corridor, down three flights of stairs, out the hospital doors, east to Seventeenth Avenue, north to 81st street. He did not stop running until he was on his own block. He crouched outside his building and panted.

Half an hour later he watched his father park the blue Chevrolet across the street and then sit motionless in the driver's seat for a minute. When Mr. Brogan finally got out of the car he stared at Monty for a long time over the roof of the Chevrolet. He started to cross the street, turned back, unlocked the passenger door, and reached inside. He slammed the door and checked both ways for oncoming traffic, the red plastic fireman's helmet in his hand.

TWENTY-TWO

THE PARKED CARS lining the avenue look like scoops of vanilla ice cream, glistening below the streetlights. The awnings of the buildings, fringed with icicles, creak beneath the weight of the snow. The sidewalk plane trees, pin oaks, and Callery pears in their little squares of soil stand motionless in the still, clear air, the curves of each branch precisely traced by curves of snow. The avenue looks unreal to Jakob: too white, too silent, like an abandoned mansion, its furniture draped with white sheets. The snow has stopped falling.

Doyle, off his leash, charges down the middle of the street, carving a trail through the foot-deep powder, a drop of ink rolling down a blank page. Monty follows behind, twirling circles with the leash, his ruined shoes squeaking with each step. Jakob and Slattery walk side by side, a few feet farther back. Jakob tries to step carefully into the hollows of Monty's footprints, the tramped-down snow, but mimicking Monty's longer stride is awkward, ruining Jakob's rhythm. Slattery wades forward, his pant legs soaked from the knees down.

Ten minutes before, the three of them had marched up the narrow staircase to Monty's apartment and sat in silence in the dark living room, nobody willing to say a word. The light spilled out below the door of the bedroom but Monty did not go in there; he sat on the floor, his back against the radiator, scratching behind Doyle's mangled ear. Jakob pictured Naturelle lying in bed, eyes open, waiting. For some reason the image stabbed at Jakob. He wondered if she knew that Monty had fucked another woman back at the club, if she cared.

Monty finally stood up and said, "Let's take Doyle for a walk. One last walk with Doyle," and the four of them trudged back out to the snow.

Jakob listens to the sounds of Slattery's heavy footsteps; he feels his friend's exhaustion, his frustration. In a strange way it comforts him to see how bad Slattery looks, how miserable. His face is troubled, gloomy, and Jakob feels a great surge of affection for him, to see him so wretched on account of another. Slattery's a good man after all. Not a sweetheart, but a man you'd want on your side when the troubles come.

Still, he'll look fine by the weekend, thinks Jakob. We'll both look fine. In a few hours, while Monty is riding the bus to Otisville, Slattery can crawl into bed, the shades pulled down, sleep until Sunday, watch the Super Bowl at a friend's apartment: bowls of popcorn and nachos on the coffee table; happy, well-fed people piled on the sofa, lounging on the floor, drinking beers in the kitchen; everybody cheering when the good guys score.

The four of them march down the middle of the avenue, a crew of jaywalkers stomping past red lights on the eastern edge of the hushed island. The only vehicle on the road is a snowplow half a mile south, its yellow lights flashing. Jakob wonders how far he would walk through the snow before protesting. Monty could lead them to the Gulf of Mexico and they would tramp wearily behind, unaware of the sand and shells beneath their feet.

At 86th Street they cross into Carl Schurz Park, past the fenced-in gingko trees. Doyle spots a squirrel sitting on its hind legs by a garbage can; they stare at each other for a moment and then Doyle pounces, kicking up snow. Jakob is relieved when the squirrel makes it to an oak tree and climbs to safety. Doyle sits below, tongue hanging from the side of his mouth, staring sadly up through the branches.

They follow Monty up a cascading series of steps—the actual steps hard to discern in the deep snow and weak light—and along a trail that winds past red maples, lampposts, and park benches. When they get to the playground, Jakob taps Slattery's elbow and gestures: *This is where he's taking us.* They have heard the story before, of how Monty and Naturelle first met on the swings. But Monty doesn't even slow down; he leads them past the swings, the sandboxes, the monkey bars, past the basketball courts and roller-hockey rink, onto the esplanade that runs for miles along the East River.

Jakob has never been on the esplanade at night. Now he understands why Monty wanted to come. Across the river lies Queens, and Queens before sunrise is beautiful: red antennae lights winking to warn pilots; the Pepsi sign glowing in neon script over the bottling plant; white clouds rising from the smokestacks like genies, bulging and blustering, ready to grant three wishes to the good people of Astoria. Behind Queens the sky is beginning to brighten, a pale blue band at the eastern horizon that darkens progressively into the black above Manhattan.

Jakob brushes snow off the iron rail of the balustrade, leans against it, and stares into the river. A string of yellow lights quivers beneath the water, and Jakob shudders, imagining a legion of drowned men bearing torches, all of them standing silent vigil on the riverbed. He knows it's nothing but the reflection of electric lights fixed to the suspension cables of the Queensboro Bridge, but Jakob can't shake the image of bloated, eyeless bodies waiting below the water.

"Look at the lighthouse," says Monty, pointing with one gloved hand to the stone tower on the northern tip of Roosevelt Island. "They should fix it up, get it working again. Be nice to come out here and see it working. No tugboats around. Crews are probably stuck in their driveways in Staten Island." Monty laughs. "I figure all the tugboat guys live in Staten Island. I don't know why."

"Those guys make good money," says Slattery, who has joined them by the balustrade. "They have one of the best unions in the city. Them and the crane operators."

"It would be good to work a tugboat," says Monty. "Hauling barges around, being out on the river all day. Get the radio tuned to a game, you know, just smoking and watching the city roll by."

Slattery shakes his head. "You'd be watching the city so much you'd run into it."

"So what do you think," says Monty, turning to face Jakob. "You ready for Mr. Doyle?"

Jakob watches the dog rolling in the snow, pawing at the air. "He likes the snow."

"He'll be good for you, Jake. Nobody's going to break into your apartment, that's for sure. And girls love Doyle. Take him for walks, you'll see. It's a certain type of girl that goes for Doyle. It's the funky ones. Look at him. It's the ones that like old beat-up tough guys. What time you got?"

"Quarter past seven."

"Quarter past seven." Monty drums a quick riff on the iron rail and hauls himself over the balustrade with one motion. He stands on the narrow ledge, the backs of his knees against the rail, the river below him.

"Wait," says Slattery, holding his hands up. "What are you doing? Monty, what are you doing?"

Doyle—belly down in the snow, panting—stares up at his master. Jakob's mouth hangs open, the words caught in his throat.

Monty watches the dark water flowing beneath him. "What do you think, about forty feet down? What are you worried about? I can't kill myself jumping forty feet. Unless I freeze to death."

"Come on," says Slattery. "Come on, give me your hand. Don't fuck around."

"Don't fuck around? I should be serious, right?" Monty scrapes snow off the ledge with his shoe. "I'm not going in there like this. They'll eat me alive."

"Come on," says Slattery. "You're going to slip and break your neck."

For a long moment Monty says nothing, staring across the river at Queens. Finally he turns, grabs the rail of the balustrade, and vaults back to the esplanade, his feet skidding on the snow as he lands. Slattery grabs him around the waist and keeps him from falling; Doyle barks; Jakob exhales.

"I'm not going in there like this," repeats Monty, shoving Slattery away. "The minute they get a look at me, I'm gone. You got to help me out, Frank."

"Tell me how," says Slattery, bewildered.

Monty whistles for Doyle and the dog jumps to his feet and runs over, wagging the stump of his tail, his muzzle powdered with snow. Monty hooks the leash onto the dog's collar and ties the cord around a baluster, knotting it twice.

"Make me ugly," says Monty.

Slattery and Jakob look at each other.

"You told me before," says Monty. "Anything I need." He unbuttons his coat and lays it carefully atop the balustrade.

Slattery shakes his head. "I can't do that. What are you thinking, I give you a black eye and people won't fuck with you? It won't change anything."

"You think I deserve it, don't you? I blew it, right? That's what you think, I had a good chance and I blew it?"

Slattery keeps shaking his head. He backs away from Monty. "I can't hit you."

Monty stands with his feet apart, his arms crossed over his chest. He looks smaller now, without his coat on, the black wool sweater narrowing his body. "I think you can. I think you want to, a little bit. I think you've wanted to for years."

"I'm not doing it."

"You want to," says Monty, advancing on him. "Come on, Frank. You're afraid?"

Slattery holds his hands up, palms toward Monty. "Listen—"

"What are you afraid of, Frank? That I'll hit back? You're afraid

I'll get mad and hit back? That would be embarrassing, right? Big tough guy like you getting your ass kicked?"

"Come on," says Jakob. "This is crazy."

Monty turns on Jakob and points a gloved finger at him. "Who's talking to you? Who the fuck is talking to you?"

"Forget it," says Slattery. "Come on, forget all this. Let's get some breakfast."

"This all works out pretty well for you, doesn't it, Frank? Pretty convenient for you. You're going to look after Naturelle when I'm gone, right? You're going to make sure she's okay?"

"What?"

"You think she doesn't know how bad you want her? You're fucking pathetic, drooling after her all the time; you're like a dog sniffing her ass. She laughs at you, Frank. You're a joke, an old joke, and you're not even funny anymore. She's not even flattered anymore, it's gone on so long."

"All right," says Slattery quietly. "All right." He turns stiffly and walks away.

"Come on," whispers Jakob. "Monty, come on, what are you doing? Tell him you're kidding."

Monty pivots and punches Jakob hard on the cheek, the crack of gloved knuckle on bone echoing on the empty esplanade. Jakob falls back against the balustrade, clutching his face.

"*Monty,*" he says.

Monty steps closer and punches Jakob again, this time in the gut, and Jakob sinks to his knees, gasping. He covers his face with his hands, to protect himself, then hears a great groan, hears the sound of two bodies slamming into the snow. When he looks up he sees that Slattery has tackled Monty, has pinned him to the ground. Slattery holds Monty's throat with his left hand and drives his right fist into Monty's face, again and again and again and again and again.

Doyle is howling, trying to jump onto Slattery but yanked back each time by the leash. He strains forward, fangs bared, the muscles in his hind legs bunching, but his master is three feet too far.

He never quits; he keeps jumping for Slattery, keeps being yanked back by the leash.

Jakob touches the burning skin of his cheek and examines his fingers: no blood. Slattery keeps hitting Monty, the blows beginning to sound wet, Monty no longer wriggling beneath him.

"Frank," says Jakob, grabbing hold of the balustrade and pulling himself to his feet. "Frank!"

The blood puddling by Monty's head, melting through the snow and steaming in the air. The sound of a fist unmaking a face. The dog howling and battling the leash.

Jakob stumbles over to Slattery and pushes him. "Stop!"

Slattery looks up, his face wet with tears, his mouth open, a webbing of saliva between his lips.

"Okay," says Jakob. "Enough." He places his hands under the big man's arms and helps him rise.

"Oh, Jesus," says Slattery, looking down at Monty. "Oh, Jesus."

Jakob crouches and turns Monty onto his stomach and Monty coughs, a thick ribbon of blood falling from his mouth. Doyle barks madly. Jakob scoops up a handful of snow and begins gently pressing it to the side of Monty's face; he listens to make sure that Monty is breathing.

Slattery watches, speechless, bloodied hands by his side. Jakob remains crouched next to Monty, his fingers resting on the back of Monty's neck. Doyle keeps barking, over and over, the collar digging into his throat as he struggles to reach his master. A tugboat sounds its horn on the river and Jakob thinks, One crew made it to their boat.

Finally Monty shakes his head clear of the snow and begins crawling forward.

"Hold still for a minute," says Jakob. "Hold still."

When Monty tries to stand his legs collapse beneath him. Jakob wraps his arms around him before he falls and lowers him slowly back to the snow.

"Don't try to move yet."

Monty pushes himself off the ground again and this time manages to keep his balance, though he sways like a drunk. "It's okay," he mumbles, the words slurred. He turns to face his friends.

Slattery looks at him and moans, sits down heavily in the snow, his chin tucked against his chest, his right hand, slick with blood, covering his face. "Oh, Jesus."

"Hospital," says Jakob. "We need to take you to a hospital."

"No," says Monty, staggering toward them. Doyle is mewling now, stomping his paws, confused. Monty bends down unsteadily and scratches behind the dog's ear.

"Be a good boy," he says.

Slattery is still sitting in the snow, sobbing. Monty leans over and kisses his forehead.

"I'm sorry," says Monty.

Slattery rocks back and forth, hands over his face, his forehead marked with blood.

Monty turns to Jakob and touches his shoulder. "Take care of my dog."

He lifts his coat off the balustrade and walks away from them, away from the black river, the steel bridges, the stone lighthouse, away from the sun beginning to rise over Queens, away from the basketball courts, the swings in the playground, down the cascading steps and west toward home.

TWENTY-THREE

SHE SEES HIM when he's still three blocks away, a black-clad figure limping through the snow, holding his coat down by his hip. *He's alive.* She breathes in deeply, the cold air burning her throat; she reaches for the silver crucifix hanging around her neck but it's not there; it's upstairs on the night table, atop the coil of silver chain. She starts walking toward him but stops after a few steps, squinting, the early morning light flaring off the snow. Even from this distance she can tell that something is wrong. When he's a block away she realizes why he's not wearing the camel's-hair coat. He doesn't want blood to drip on it.

Blood leaks from his nose, from his mouth, from a deep gash bisecting one eyebrow. The entire left side of his face is bright red, grotesquely swollen, a thumb-length welt curling under the cheekbone. His nose is badly broken; his lower lip is split in two places; a patch of skin the size of a dollar bill has been scraped off his forehead. His throat is striped red and white.

The swelling has narrowed his eyes to slits; he doesn't see her standing by the stoop steps, wearing his old hooded sweatshirt, until he is almost upon her. When he does see her he smiles, and she has to look away for a moment, his beautiful teeth ruined, three knocked out of the bottom row, one front tooth chipped badly. He tries to say something but chokes, leans over, hands on his knees, and spits up blood.

Naturelle takes him by the hand and leads him slowly up the stoop steps, through the two entrance doors, up the narrow staircase and into their apartment. Pale sunlight shines through the windows. She sits him down on the sofa and runs into the bathroom, rummages through the medicine cabinet for the things she needs, fills a glass with cold water and returns to him, makes him drink. He tries to speak again but she shakes her head, takes the glass from him, and rests it on the coffee table. Lifting his arms above his head she pulls the black sweater off, unbuttons his shirt, and slides it over his shoulders. She runs her hands quickly over his rib cage, watching his face to see if he flinches.

She goes into the kitchen for a washcloth, fills a bowl with warm water and liquid soap, hurries back to the living room, and sits beside him. She begins gently cleaning his face, pausing when he jerks back, then leaning forward again to dab at each cut and scrape. When she wrings the washcloth above the bowl, drops of blood fall into the water and bloom. After she is satisfied that each wound is cleaned, she opens a bottle of witch hazel and wets a cotton ball. She presses the cotton lightly against the gash that splits his eyebrow; Monty shudders, his fingers gripping the edges of the sofa cushions. Eight cotton balls soaked in witch hazel lie on the coffee table when she's finished. She tapes a gauze pad over the gash. He'll need stitches, she thinks. She imagines a prison doctor roughly sewing him up while joking with the nurse. Will they handcuff him to the table?

Monty's head lolls against the back of the sofa, his battered face framed in sunlight. The night is over and he is asleep. She watches him breathing, the rise and fall of his rib cage, the tremor of pulse at the base of his throat. She looks up at the clock on the far wall. She needs to wake him, dress him in clean clothes, take him downstairs, and find a taxi. She watches him dreaming, his eyelids fluttering, his fingers curling and uncurling, grasping for something. One more minute and she'll wake him. Give him one more minute.

TWENTY-FOUR

WHEN MONTY OPENS his eyes his father is standing before him with clenched fists.

"Who did this to you?"

Monty reaches for a glass of water and recoils when the rim touches a broken tooth. The pain is shocking, fierce and electric. Monty lowers his head and waits for the nerves to quiet, then raises the drink again and sips more carefully. When he finishes, Naturelle takes the glass from him and goes to the kitchen to re-fill it.

"Who did this to you, Monty?" his father repeats.

"What time is it?" Monty can see the clock on the far wall but can't read the hands. The room is blurred with sunlight and shadows, all the edges washed away. His father's face is a pale oval that bends and splits when he speaks.

"I'm bringing you to the hospital," says Mr. Brogan. "We can tell—"

"No," says Monty. He puts his palms down on the sofa cushions and pushes himself upright. "I need to go."

Naturelle returns with a full glass of water. She waits quietly, her eyes focused on Monty's hands.

"What time is it?" he asks again. He pulls on his shirt and buttons it crooked; Naturelle sets the glass on the coffee table and fixes him. She hands him his sweater and he slides into it, then heads for his bedroom, banging his shin against the table.

"Monty," says Mr. Brogan. Monty stops and looks at his father but Mr. Brogan says nothing else, so Monty goes into his room, looks at the unmade bed, the running tights on the floor, the bowl of plums on the bedside table beside an empty pack of cigarettes. He pulls off his wet shoes and finds an old pair of workboots in the closet, slips them on, and laces them.

He pulls out the empty suitcase from under the bed and packs what to wear on the day they free him: his midnight-blue suit, neatly folded; his suede cap-toe boots fitted with hand-carved cedar shoe trees; a black silk shirt with silver quarter moons for buttons; boxer shorts; black dress socks. He packs a string of old Spanish rosary beads that Naturelle gave him on his birthday two years ago. He packs the photograph of his mother, father, and six-year-old self standing before the lit Christmas tree.

He returns to the living room and leaves the suitcase by the front door. "I'll say goodbye here," he says. He goes to Naturelle and gathers her in his arms. He holds her for a long time before letting go. She smiles up at him, her lips pressed tightly together. The skin around her eyes is dark and swollen from lack of sleep. She blinks and looks away but Monty watches her for a moment more. She seems very young right now, all her makeup washed away, her long black hair tied back in a schoolgirl's ponytail.

He approaches his father but Mr. Brogan shakes his head.

"How you planning on getting to the Port Authority?"

"Subway."

"You won't make it. Trains are barely running right now. I'll drive you to Otisville. Jesus, look what they did to you."

"Come on, Dad, go easy on me. I'll take a taxi."

"There won't be any taxis," says Naturelle. "Let him take you to a hospital."

"You don't trust my driving?" asks Mr. Brogan, trying to smile. "I got chains on the tires and everything."

"I don't want it like this. You're making it harder. Let me walk away, Dad. It's easier that way."

"What's easy about it, Monty? Easy? My God, you don't understand, do you? You don't have any idea." He touches Monty's cheeks very lightly with his fingertips. "Let me drive you there. I need to see where it is anyway, for visits. Okay, buddy? Help me out."

Monty blinks and then nods. "No hospitals," he says.

Mr. Brogan kisses Naturelle on the cheek and she embraces the older man, wrapping her arms around his winter parka and hugging him very hard. When she releases him he walks to the front door and opens it, picks up the suitcase, and leaves the apartment without closing the door. Monty stands still, looking at Naturelle. They listen to his father's footsteps echoing in the stairwell.

"Wait a second," she says. She goes into the kitchen and he waits, rocking back and forth on his boot heels, his eyes closed. The faucet in the kitchen is dripping slowly, each drop a distant handclap. When Naturelle comes back she gives him a plastic bag filled with ice cubes and makes him hold it against the side of his face. They don't move for a moment, her hand on top of his hand, the bag of ice pressed to his jaw.

He wants her to grab him, to whisper that she knows a place to hide where no one will ever find them. He wants her to promise that she'll follow, that she'll find a job in Otisville and come to visit every week. He wants her to say that seven years will pass like a night's bad dream, that he will wake to find her arms around him, that a lifetime is waiting for them around the bend.

Naturelle says nothing and Monty says nothing. Finally he nods and turns away, closing the door softly behind him. He unknots the plastic bag and dumps the ice down the stairwell, watching the cubes glitter and disappear before clattering on the linoleum three floors below. He balls the empty bag and pockets it.

Downstairs Mr. Brogan's car is double-parked in front of the building, his hazard lights blinking. The roof of the old Honda is crowned with snow but the windshield and rear window have been swept clean. Mr. Brogan opens the passenger door and Monty eases carefully into the seat, then leans over to unlock his father's side.

They wait for a minute until the engine is purring smoothly and warm air is flowing through the vents. "FDR is closed," says Mr. Brogan. "I figured we'd go up First Avenue, take the Triborough, catch 87 up to Route 17, and then 211 takes us right into Otisville. Easy drive, except for the snow." Monty doesn't respond so Mr. Brogan continues. "I saw a bad accident on the BQE. A tow truck flipped over. They were going to tow the tow truck, I guess, but they had to get it on its feet first. Its wheels, I mean."

Monty rubs the corners of his eyes and his fingers find crust there. He picks away the dried blood. His father sees what he's doing and hands him a red handkerchief from his coat pocket.

"It's clean," says Mr. Brogan, studying the side of his son's face. "Jesus, look what they did to you. I'll tell you what, Monty, you're going to be okay. The false teeth they put in now, you can't tell the difference. How's your nose?"

"Broken."

"Broken nose, that's character. It looks bad now, I know it, but when all the swelling goes down it's going to be okay. Don't worry, when you come home, you're still the best-looking kid in Bensonhurst. They sure gave you a licking, though. How many were there?"

"I don't know, Dad. A bunch of them."

They drive up First Avenue, the tire chains chanting steadily: *deh-deh-leh-deh-deh, deh-deh-leh-deh-deh*. Each time Monty presses the handkerchief against his eyes, pain flares along the bridge of his nose. But he can see a little better now. He looks out the window and watches the city roll by.

The white clouds above them are cracked here and there with blue. The streetlights are still on, glowing weakly in the morning air. A mustachioed man stands on a corner, holding a cigarette in gloved fingers, his snow shovel resting in the crook of his elbow. A woman wearing a man's overcoat, the hem brushing against the toes of her galoshes, shakes salt on the sidewalk in front of a shuttered butcher shop. Two young boys drag their sleds behind them, huffing and puffing with exaggerated fatigue, their breath rising above their bright-red faces. A man and woman wearing matching green parkas load their skis into the rack on their car's roof. A newspaper vendor sits on a blue milk crate, sipping coffee from a paper cup, while his curly-haired son snaps icicles from the kiosk's eaves. A police officer, hands on his hips, stares under the opened hood of his cruiser while his partner leans against the driver's-side door and laughs into his walkie-talkie.

At a red light on 96th Street, Monty looks up at the city bus idling noisily alongside them. A little boy in the backseat, wearing a white knit skullcap, waves at Monty. Monty waves back. The boy taps on the window and Monty reads the letters finger-drawn on the frosted glass: *moT.* It takes Monty a moment to figure it out. Then he smiles as well as he can and draws on his own window: *Monty.* Before he can cross the *t* the bus pulls away and Monty watches it go, trailing exhaust in its wake.

"Give me the word," says Mr. Brogan, "and I'll take a left turn."

"Left turn to where?"

"We can take the George Washington Bridge. Wherever you want." Mr. Brogan drives carefully, hands on the wheel at ten o'clock and two o'clock, squinting into the slush ahead for potholes. "We'll get you stitched up somewhere and go west, find a nice little town—"

"Dad."

"I'm saying if you want. If that's what you want, I'll do it. We'll drive and keep driving. Stop in Chicago for a Cubs game. I've always wanted to see Wrigley Field. Maybe we can go to the Grand Canyon, take a few pictures. We'll find a little town somewhere, find a bar, and I'll buy us drinks. I haven't had a drink in nineteen years, but I'll have one with you. And then I'll leave. I'll tell you, Don't ever write me, don't ever come visit. I'll tell you I believe in God's Kingdom and I believe I'll be with you again, and your mother. But not in this lifetime."

Monty runs his tongue over the splintered roots of his missing teeth. The left side of his face feels as if it had been pressed onto the red-hot coils of an electric stovetop. He looks at his father and sees the determination on the man's face, eyes unblinking, muscles in his jaw bunched behind his cheek like a wad of chewing tobacco.

"They'll take your bar from you."

"Jesus." Mr. Brogan shakes his head. "My bar? They can take my bar to hell. You think my bar is more important to me? If you say the word, Monty, we go."

"They'll find me. Sooner or later—"

"You know how they find people, Monty? They find them when they come home. People run away but they usually come back, and that's when they get caught. So you go and you never come back. You get a job somewhere, a job that pays cash, a boss who doesn't ask questions, and you make a new life, and you never come back."

"I can't get away from it, Dad. Okay? I'm stuck with it, it's going to happen. Please? Just take me to Otisville."

But for the space of a mile, as the old car wheezes and hacks through the slush, as the tire chains chant *deh-deh-leh-deh-deh, deh-deh-leh-deh-deh*, Monty closes his eyes and unleashes the temptation, lets it run free in his mind. He has thought these thoughts a thousand times, but they've never been so pure as now, when a left turn westward can make them reality. Drive west and keep on driving, over the Hudson River, through the New Jersey suburbs, through states Monty cannot map, whatever lies west of New Jersey—Pennsylvania, maybe, and then Ohio? He imagines the hills and shivering cows, red farmhouses and white church spires, the black road carving through the middle of it all. He imagines miles of cornfields and wonders what cornfields look like in winter. He imagines the desert, a vastness of sand and wind-carved mesas, pitchfork cacti lining the roadside. A dusty town lost somewhere in this West, a bar with a sign on the window: HELP WANTED. Hiring on to barback, washing the glasses, sweeping the floor, sleeping on a cot in the back room. Going to the nearest city and finding the right people, buying a forged driver's license and birth certificate. The bar owner would have a beautiful daughter, and at first he would warn Monty that the girl was not for him, but he would watch how hard Monty worked, how the glasses sparkled, how the floor shined; he would promote Monty to bartender and marvel at the place's growing popularity; he would admit to his friends that here was an honest man, a man you could trust with the till, a man who never pocketed what wasn't his. The bar owner's daughter, black-haired and black-eyed, would smile at Monty from across the room; she would keep her lips closed to hide her crooked teeth. He would buy her a turquoise-and-silver necklace with six months' savings, and she would cry as she unwrapped it; she would bury her face against his chest and wet his shirt with her tears. They would drive to the nearest river and lay their clothes on clay-colored rocks and step into the cold cold water, hand in hand, an eagle cutting figure-eights in the sky far above them. On a dry summer evening a brush fire would start in the western hills and quickly gather force, marching toward town, the jackrabbits and armadillos fleeing before it. Everyone would pray for rain but none would fall. Monty would join the volunteer firefighters and battle the blaze for three days and three nights, chopping down trees and clearing brush for a firebreak around the perimeter of the town, hosing the rooftops as the citizens packed their cars and prepared to flee. The volunteers' efforts would be rewarded, the wind direction would change, and the town would be saved. A parade would be held on Main Street to celebrate the victory and thank the heroes; Monty would roll by in the mayor's convertible and wave to the cheering crowd. One day the bar owner would pull Monty aside and ask him if he loved the man's daughter, and Monty would tell him, Yes, with all my heart, and the bar owner would say, I'd be proud to call you son. Monty would shake the man's hand and they'd have the wedding that Sunday. The bride would walk down the nave in her mother's white dress, and Monty would wait for her, his new friends by his side, electricians and truck drivers and

firemen and the high school basketball coach—Monty helps him
in the winters, running the kids through drills, playing in scrim-
mages sometimes but never showing off, because these are just
kids, desert kids, they dribble slow and have no left, but Monty
never steals the ball, he never ever steals the ball. He would kiss his
wife and the priest would smile and pronounce the benedictions.
Soon they'd have children, green-eyed sons and black-eyed daugh-
ters. The kids would be country, going fishing during the long
summer afternoons, riding horses through narrow canyons, attend-
ing church every Sunday in their blazers and ties and gingham
dresses. They would grow up smart and kind and cheerful, they
would get good grades and go to college, they would become doctors and engineers and teachers, they would have their own fami-
lies and come home for the holidays, all their black-haired children
in tow. And on one of these days—make it the Fourth of July—
after the fireworks had boomed and spangled the sky, after the last
ear of corn had been chewed down to the cob and the last crust of
pie gobbled up by the littlest girl, after the babies had been put in
their cribs and everyone else had gathered in the living room,
black-and-white photographs of the past forty years hanging on
the walls—Monty's photographs, for this is his hobby and he's become expert at it; his friends tell him he should have a show
somewhere but he never does—Monty would stand in front of
them and tell a story. Everyone would be quiet, listening, because
Grandpa isn't a big talker; this is a rare thing happening. The
smaller ones, sitting cross-legged on the floor, big-eyed and open-
mouthed, would stare up at him. His children would listen carefully, exchanging glances once in a while and shaking their heads,
for what they hear sounds impossible, but they know it's true, all of
it, every word. Monty's wife would watch her husband, not hearing the words because she knows the story. He told her the night
before their wedding. He told her he would understand if she
never wanted to see him again, that if she wanted he would buy a
bus ticket and leave that night and never come back. His black-
eyed wife would watch him and remember that night, and re-

member what she said: Stay, stay with me. Monty would tell the story to his family and the rest of the world would be still, his pit bull on the front porch would quit barking, the crickets and coyotes and owls would hush, and Monty would tell his story, of who he is and where he came from. He would tell the whole thing and then listen to the silence. You see? he would ask. You see how lucky we are to be here? All of it, all of you, came so close to never happening. This life came so close to never happening.